# MAYA'S CHOICE

Earl Sewell

# MAYA'S CHOICE

KIMANI
tru
™

Recycling programs
for this product may
not exist in your area.

MAYA'S CHOICE

ISBN-13: 978-0-373-22998-7

www.kimanipress.com

**Printed in U.S.A.**

# Acknowledgments

To my readers who have fallen in love with the Keysha's Drama series. It is my hope that you will find an equally meaningful relationship with Maya, Keysha's best friend, whom you've previously met in my prior book, *Myself and I.* This is the first installment of the Keysha and Friends series, and it holds a proud position in my heart.

I want to say thank you to the following people for all of their help with my endless questions about Mexican culture: Maria Velasquez of Orozco Community Academy, Esperanza Gonzalez and Adrianna Galvin. Thank you for taking time out of your busy schedules to provide me with invaluable insight.

To Glenda Howard, who has stood with me and been a champion of my career and this new series from the beginning. Thank you so much for your belief in my work and talent.

To Linda Wilson, who has been my right arm during the production phase of my last several novels. Thank you for always being available and for never complaining, even when I come to you with my hair on fire.

To my family, Annette and Candice, as always. Thanks for putting up with me and my madness during the production of this novel.

I have to send out an extra-special thank-you to Kim Boyd, Kimberly Cox, Lisa Walsh, Renee Simms, Andrea Nixon, Antoinette McClellan-Brown, Michelle Van Allen and Joy Lewis. All of you have been champions of my teen titles. Without your help and support I know my series would not have become as popular as it has.

To all who have discovered my teen titles and have either shared or recommended them to young readers, thank you so much for helping me spread the word.

Please feel free to drop me a line at earl@earlsewell.com and please put the title of my book in the subject line so that I know your message to me is not spam. Make sure you check out www.earlsewell.net and www.myspace.com/earlsewell. You can also hit me up on Facebook and Twitter. Just type in my name and you should be able to find me with little difficulty.

For my Aunt Mini Sewell-Franklin

"You've always understood
the power and importance of our family history."

# one

## MAYA

I'd just sat down in front of the television in the basement and was about to watch *True Blood,* when I glanced at my leg and the orthopedic boot I was wearing and remembered that I'd left some new sandals that I'd picked up from the mall in the trunk of my mother's car. The patent leather yellow sandals were a bit out of my price range, but I had promised them to myself as a reward once my leg healed. I rose to my feet, strapped my foot into my shoe boot and made my way toward the garage door. Thankfully, I wouldn't have to hobble around in the boot for much longer, because soon it would be coming off for good. I walked into the laundry room and opened a side door that led outside, then made my way to the garage. As I opened the garage door, I thought about the day my cast was removed.

I was sitting in the doctor's office with my dad, who'd taken the day off so that he could take me to my appointment. The television in the waiting room was tuned into the *Wendy Williams Show.* Wendy was in a good mood, dishing out all of the celebrity gossip on everyone from Charlie

Sheen to Tiger Woods. As my dad watched the show with me, he began shaking his head.

"What's wrong?" I asked.

"I'm trying to figure out who this Snooki lady is," he said, focusing all of his attention on Wendy, who was holding up an enlarged picture of Snooki.

"She's one of the stars on a reality TV show called *Jersey Shore*," I informed him.

"Well, Snooki is wearing the same type of hair pouf your mom used to wear back in the 1980s. It's funny how fashion and hairstyles come and go." My dad spoke confidently, as though he was down on all teenage trends.

Other people in the waiting room began snickering at his silly comment. When I rolled my eyes, my dad cracked a smile.

A nurse appeared from behind a door and called my name. "Maya Rogers."

"Yes, that's me," I answered as I prepared to stand. My dad and I made our way back to the examination room and waited for the doctor.

"Hello, Mr. Rogers. Maya, how are you doing?" Dr. Barrios asked when she walked into the room. She was a woman in her mid-fifties with black shoulder-length hair, tanned skin and a warm smile. My dad gave a nod in greeting before taking a seat in the guest chair.

"I'd be doing much better if I didn't have this dang cast on," I said with blunt honesty. "My leg itches all of the time and it's really annoying."

"Well, today we're going to cut the cast off, take an X-ray and see how you're healing," she said as she sat down on a stool and rolled over to my leg. She removed the sock that I had covering my toes.

"I like that color you've painted your toes," she complimented me.

"Oh, thank you," I said as I thought about my best friend, Keysha, who had painted them neon-pink.

Dr. Barrios then said, "Wiggle your toes for me." I moved my toes as she'd requested.

"Good. Okay. Let me cut you out of that thing."

Dr. Barrios used a saw to remove the cast from my leg. I was so freaking happy to have that thing taken off. When I saw my leg it was ashy-white and very dry. There was a nasty-looking blister that had formed at my heel where my foot would sweat and rub against the cast. My leg also looked smaller than the other one and was very sensitive to touch. It also smelled musty from being confined to the cast and was rather hairy.

"Ewww," I said, touching my leg and wanting to shave right away.

"I know what you're thinking, and if I were you I'd wait for the skin to become a little less sensitive before attempting to shave or use hair remover."

"My leg is as hairy as a man's," I griped, but had no intention to irritate it more than it already was.

"Well, let's go and get that X-ray to see how the bone has healed up." I hobbled over to a nearby wheelchair and sat down. I told my dad that I'd be back soon as I was being wheeled away.

After taking a look at the X-ray Dr. Barrios came back into the room where my father and I were waiting.

"Well, Maya, you're certainly an amazing young woman who has the ability to heal up very quickly," she said, smiling as she placed the X-ray on a light box where my father and I could see it.

"That's such good news," my father said. "But what exactly does that mean?"

"It means that your daughter is a resilient young lady. She doesn't need the cast anymore." Dr. Barrios looked directly at me. "I'm going to have you fitted for an orthopedic boot and sign you up for some physical therapy so that you can get the strength back in your leg."

"Can I stand up?" I asked.

"Yes, but don't be surprised if your leg feels a little funny, and don't put your weight on it." Totally excited, I didn't even let her finish her sentence. I rose up out of the wheelchair and placed most of the pressure on my good leg before slowly balancing my weight on my other leg. It was a little disappointing to realize that my leg wasn't strong enough to support me just yet.

I grabbed the bag I was searching for out of the trunk of the car and headed back inside the house. I made my way back toward the television and saw that my younger sister, Anna, held the remote control and was about to sit down in the La-Z-Boy chair. As nicely as I could I told her that I was actually there first and was about to watch *True Blood* before she had come in. Anna, without so much as giving it a second thought, offered up an explosive response.

"I don't care what you say. When I came in you were nowhere near the television—so, too bad. I'm about to watch

*America's Best Dance Crew*." Anna held the television remote, aimed it and flipped the channel to her show.

"I only went to the garage for a few minutes and planned on watching television down here. Besides, you know it takes me a little longer to do everything with this orthopedic boot on," I said, speaking calmly.

"Do I look like a Maya mind reader? Am I supposed to know your every thought? Am I supposed to know where you are every second of the day? I don't think so," she said unapologetically before plopping down on the La-Z-Boy and turning up the volume. I released an aggravated sigh as I tried to keep my temper in check. Anna and I would get along so much better if she were to just drop off the face of the earth. I'm sure my parents would be the only two people on the planet who'd miss her, because I certainly wouldn't. Anna was stubborn, hardheaded and, most of all, annoying. Unfortunately for me, Anna had the unique ability to get under my skin by just breathing.

"Why don't you just go watch it in another room? Why do you have to be down here?" I tried to reason with her as I braced myself against the back of the sofa.

"For the same reason you want to watch your show in here—because this is the biggest television in the house." Anna folded her arms and repositioned herself in the seat as if she were a boulder that would not be moved easily.

"Anna, if you don't change back the channel I'm going to make you regret it." I raised my voice, hoping to frighten her.

"Please! What are you going to do, broke-leg mountain?

Hop over here and try to beat me down? All I'd have to do is push you and you'd fall faster than rain."

"I bet I won't. Come on. Try it. I dare you!" I encouraged Anna to try her luck. She'd never won a fight against me and, even with a leg that was still healing up, I wasn't going to allow her to win. I was more than willing to fight dirty and draw blood with my teeth, if it came to that.

"Don't think that I won't get up and do it," Anna snapped at me. It was clear, at least in my mind, that she had become overconfident by my somewhat hindered mobility. A part of me was willing to drop the conversation and watch the show in another room, but when Anna stuck her tongue out at me I immediately changed my mind. It was about respect now, and I had to place her in check. I tucked my crutches beneath my armpits and swung myself around the sofa so I could snatch the remote from her hand.

"Why are you two in here shouting at each other?" My mother, Raven, walked into the room carrying a laundry hamper filled with dirty clothes. She was a beautiful Mexican woman with round cheeks, a perfect smile and brown hair. She was meticulous about the care of her skin, which always appeared absolutely flawless, even without makeup. She was tall, about five-eight and, for a woman in her forties with three children, she was in excellent shape. My friend Keysha once told me that my mom reminded her of the actress Eva Longoria. My mom kept in shape through a combination of dieting and teaching Zumba classes on the weekend at a nearby health club.

"Because I was in here first and..." Anna suddenly rose

to her feet and stood directly in front of me, slightly bumping me before I could finish what I was saying.

"No, she wasn't, Mom. When I came in, she was nowhere to be found. When I turned on the television she showed up, acting all bossy for no reason at all." Anna heatedly presented her version of events.

"That's not true. I asked you nicely."

"Girls. I don't want to hear it. Can there be at least one full day where I don't have to get a phone call at work or come home and listen to you two bickering? You two fight more than I did with your aunt."

I hobbled from behind Anna and pleaded my case. "Mom, she knows how hard it is for me to get around. She could at least be considerate and let me watch my program in here. She's only doing this to annoy me."

"That's a lie. My time is too valuable to be wasting it on you," Anna blurted out.

"You know what, keep interrupting me and I'm going to kill you just like Cain killed Abel," I threatened my sister.

"Maya!" My mother raised her voice at me. "You're older and supposed to be more mature. You can't go around letting every little thing irritate you."

"But…" I wasn't about to give up.

"Who has the remote now?" my mother asked.

"I do." Anna held it up to show her.

"Then you get to watch what you want. Maya, go watch your show in another room." My mom resolved our conflict before continuing on to the laundry room.

"I hate you!" I turned and snarled at Anna.

"The feeling is mutual," she immediately responded back.

"I still hear bickering. It had better end now, or else!" Mom shouted out from the laundry room.

"This isn't over," I whispered through clenched teeth.

"Talk to the hand." Anna placed her palm in front of my face.

"That line is so old and played out. You're lucky, because if I wasn't in this boot I'd twist your fingers off," I said brazenly. As I was about to move away from her, Anna rotated her wrist and flipped up her middle finger. I lowered my eyelids to slits, wishing I had the ability of a superhero to shoot deadly flames from my eyes and burn her to a crisp.

"If you keep standing there you'll miss your show," Anna said.

As best as I could I made my way back to the living room, where there was a smaller television. As I watched the show, for some reason I can't fully explain I began to feel sorry for myself and started crying. My emotions seemed to overtake me without warning. I thought about how my leg had gotten broken at a house party that had gotten out of control and turned into a stampede. I thought about how my boyfriend, Misalo, had rescued me from getting trampled and how my parents now forbade me to see him. If that wasn't bad enough, with a broken leg I had automatically lost my job as a lifeguard, which I truly loved. I sighed, wiped away my tears and tried to force myself to stop sobbing.

"What's wrong with you?" My father, Herman, walked into the house through the garage door. He was casually dressed in denim shorts, brown summer sandals and a black polo shirt that my mother had recently picked up for him. My father stood about six-three, had smooth, brown skin like the actor Idris Elba and low-cut black hair that was turning gray. My father liked to work out and was stout with muscular arms, a broad chest and a little bit of a bloated belly. My mother would immediately get on his case if she felt his stomach was beginning to look too much like a Buddha belly. Lately he'd been trying to break his habit of eating at his two favorite fast-food restaurants, Sharks fried fish and Popeyes fried chicken, but he hadn't been that successful.

"Nothing," I answered as I tried to hide my tears. My father sat next to me and placed a bag filled with fried catfish from Sharks on an end table.

"Man, that smells good," I said.

"Do you want some? I got enough for everyone."

"You know Mom isn't going to eat that," I said with a smile.

"Well, that just means there will be more for you and me. I got a family-size side order of coleslaw and French fries, too." He picked up the bag and headed toward the kitchen. A few moments later he returned with a plate for me resting atop a food tray.

"How does your leg feel?" he asked before stepping away to grab his own plate.

"It itches like crazy." I placed a morsel of the fried fish in my mouth. "This tastes so good."

"Well, in two days you'll have another doctor's appointment, and hopefully you've completely healed up."

"I can't wait. I'm dying to get out of this boot and I'm tired of going to physical therapy," I said.

"Well, I hope this experience has taught you a lesson about the type of people you've been hanging around. Especially that boy, Misalo. He's no good for you, Maya. He's nothing but trouble."

"Dad, how can you say that? Misalo took me to prom and nothing happened. You've got it all twisted. Misalo saved me," I said, trying to once again convince him that he should be thanking my boyfriend and not condemning him.

"True. He did take you to prom, but while you were still getting dressed he and I had a little conversation. I made sure that from then on forward, if he wanted to continue dating you, he'd better bring you back home in the same condition that you left in. He promised me that he would, but that promise has been broken."

"But, Daddy, it wasn't his fault," I said, unwilling to allow Misalo's courage to go unrecognized. "Had he not protected me, things could have been worse."

"If you believe his bringing you home with a broken leg is protection, then I need to do a better job of showing you how a man is supposed to treat a woman."

"Daddy, the place was way too crowded. There were people everywhere," I explained once again.

"Didn't you tell me that there was a dogfight going on in the house?"

"Yes," I answered him.

"And did you want to see a dogfight?" He met my gaze with his own.

"No," I answered with reluctance.

"And who convinced you to go into the basement to see it anyway?"

I lowered my eyes to the floor. "Misalo," I whispered.

"So, not only did you go to an unsupervised party—

without the permission of your mother or myself, I might add—but Misalo, who apparently shares the same interests as Michael Vick and who supposedly cares for you so much, persuaded you to watch a violent and inhumane dogfight."

"Daddy, you're twisting it around!" I raised my voice.

"How am I twisting it around? That is the truth as you told it to your mother and I. Am I correct?" I could feel my father's judgmental glare heating up the side of my face. I turned to meet his gaze once again.

"Yes. But it wasn't like that. Misalo…"

My father cut me off. "Misalo was more interested in saving himself than he was with protecting you. Once all of the pushing started, he knew that if he tripped over you everyone would step on his back and crush not only you but him, as well." By the tone of Dad's voice I knew that he'd gotten irritated.

"But—" My father tossed the palm of his hand up, which made me go silent.

"He went into survival mode, Maya, just like you did. You wanted to get up. Did you care about what was happening to other people around you?"

"No," I answered. "I just wanted them to allow me to get up."

"A man, or boy for that matter, who cares for his woman or girl doesn't drag her to violent dogfights. That's like me dragging your mother to the front lines when I served in the Gulf War. Just to take a look at the horror and brutality of it all. If he's interested in that type of cruelty, his thirst for violence may end up turning on you. Do you understand what I'm getting at?" he asked.

"No!" I snapped because I wasn't able to change his perception of Misalo. "He was just curious, Dad."

"And his curiosity led to you having a broken leg," he quickly fired back.

"I'm not hungry anymore," I said tearfully.

"All the tears in the world aren't going to change my mind about him."

"I just want to go lay down," I said glumly. My father rose to his feet and then helped me to mine. I made my way to the staircase and walked up with the support of the rail. I entered my bedroom and closed the door. I went to my bed, got comfortable and glared at the ceiling. All I could see were images of Misalo desperately trying to free my leg from being completely crushed.

I can't remember when I drifted off to sleep, but I awoke to the sound of my cell phone ringing. I'd set up a special ringtone for my best friend, Keysha, so I knew right away that it was her calling.

"Hey, girl. How are you doing?" she asked, sounding more jovial than I was feeling.

"Fine," I answered.

"Ooo. You don't sound fine. What happened?" Keysha asked.

"Life," I continued with the one-word answers.

"Okay." Keysha paused. "Is this going to be like pulling teeth or are you going to talk to me?" she asked.

"I don't want to talk about my problems right now. What are you doing?" I asked.

"I'm just leaving work. The pool was supercrowded today.

I had to kick out two seventh-grade boys who were trying to drown each other."

"Who was at the pool today? Anyone I know?" I asked.

"Yes. Misalo was there and I have a message for you from him." I immediately perked up.

"He said that he misses you and he can't wait to see you. So, being the good friend that I am to both of you guys, I have taken it upon myself to help you see each other."

"I can't. My parents won't allow him to come anywhere near me." I reminded her of my dilemma.

"That's why you have me. I came up with a brilliant idea that should work," Keysha said enthusiastically.

"What have you been plotting?" I asked, pressing the phone closer to my ear.

"Okay. On my next day off, tell your parents that you want to come over to my house and hang out with me for the day. You can have them drop you off on their way to work. Then when my parents leave for their jobs, we can invite Misalo over. You guys could be together all day."

"And where will you be?" I asked.

"Minding my own business." Keysha laughed.

I popped my fingers. "I have an even better idea."

"What?" Keysha asked.

"I'll invite Misalo over to my house while my parents are at work," I said, not knowing why I hadn't thought of it before.

"But what if one of them comes home early or something?" Keysha asked.

"Please, both of my parents call me all day long to make sure I'm doing fine. They always call home when they're on their way. Besides, I'll have Misalo out of here long before they get back."

"Well, okay. If you're cool with that I'm cool with it."

"Can you give Misalo the message for me?" I asked.

"Why don't you just call him yourself?"

"Because I don't want my dad, or anyone else for that matter, to overhear me talking to him. You know how thin the walls are in my house, and for some reason the heating ducts have the ability to carry conversations through the walls," I explained.

"Okay. I'll do it now," Keysha assured me.

"You're such a good friend." I smiled as I turned over on my bed.

"Hey, you were there for me when I went through all of that drama with my ex-boyfriend Wesley, so the least I can do is be here for you."

"Since we're speaking of ex-boyfriends, have you heard from Jerry or Wesley?" I asked.

"Girl, I'll have to tell you about those tragedies later. I'm walking in the front door right now. I'll call you back in a few minutes once I've talked with Misalo," Keysha said before she hung up the phone. I wondered what kind of crazy drama was going on with Keysha, but even more exciting than that was the thought of finally seeing Misalo. My heart raced at the thought of just seeing his face.

# two

## VIVIANA

I've never really thought much about my future because I'm too busy trying to survive the present. I suppose that's why I really don't give a damn about anything. I mean, what's the point in caring or trying when you only end up hurt or deeply disappointed. This truth has been proven to me time and again. So, I choose to live day by day and deal with the trash life throws at me. That's what living is all about anyway, right? One screwed-up dilemma after another and no one really caring about it unless it impacts their world in some way. That's what I've learned, and for the most part, that's the way I see my life. No one really gives me much thought, until they have to deal with me.

My mother has a weakness for bad boys. Not the would-be kind of thug who only pretends to be hard core, but the real deal. The men she dates have to have a rap sheet at least a page long. They also need to have a thousand chicken heads after them, be as dumb as Flavor Flav is ugly, and have count-less tattoos. A short temper is a must, along with no desire to live what most of society would call a productive lifestyle. I don't know why she's fascinated with men like that. She just is. If I had to guess, though, I think she believes that if she loves them hard enough, she'll be able to change them into someone more worthwhile than who they are, and perhaps just as loving as her. So far, her love hasn't transformed any of them, but it hasn't stopped her from trying.

My mother, Salena, and I don't get along very well for a bunch of reasons, all of which are complicated and difficult to explain. We've never lived in one place for very long and we've always had to move for one reason or another. Sometimes she'd drop me off at my grandmother's house for weeks at a time until she was able to find a new apartment, get out of jail or find a new boyfriend who was willing to take us both in. I've never liked any of her male friends because all of them made my skin crawl. One guy she dated would lustfully ogle me as if I were the prize he really wanted and not my mother. It was gross to have that creep thirsty for me. When I mentioned it to my mother, she was more interested in saving her relationship than protecting me, so off to my grandmother Esmeralda's house I went.

I'd come to the conclusion that my mother only loved me when she was between men. That's when we're able to get along the best. I don't have to compete for her attention and she doesn't have to bend over backward to accommodate some jerk's every wish.

When I was thirteen, my mom and I lived in a small apartment in the Humboldt Park neighborhood of Chicago. We were able to get the place because she'd landed a job as a cook for a nursing home. It was the one time after the death of my father that she was able to find work making enough money to support us. At the time we didn't have much in the way of furnishings, just a few secondhand items that had been picked up for practically nothing from Goodwill. The apartment was drafty and needed to be repainted. The stained tan carpeting needed to be pulled up and the kitchen needed to be remodeled. In spite of everything wrong with the place, I was happy to be with her and have a place of my own to call home.

One Friday evening when I was thirteen, I walked into her bedroom just as she'd finished squeezing her oversize barrel-shaped body into an extratight, black, spaghetti-strap dress she'd recently purchased. It looked horrible on her. Her breasts looked like flapjacks, her stomach was so bloated it looked as if she'd swallowed the moon and her rear end reminded me of a sack of mashed potatoes. Even though she looked awful, I smiled and cheerfully said, "You look beautiful," as I focused on her pretty, round face, which was still pleasant to look at because she hadn't started getting deep wrinkle lines.

"Of course I do. Age hasn't caught up with me at all. I look like I'm about twenty-one years old, don't I?" she asked, fully convinced that every word she'd just spoken was an undeniable truth. My mother had just turned thirty-eight and wasn't very happy about the reality that in two years she'd be forty.

"Nineteen," I lied with a straight face—a skill that I'd already mastered.

"Ooo, that's even better. All the men at the club will be begging me for a dance tonight," she chimed gleefully, forcing her feet into a pair of worn-out high-heeled shoes.

"Can I ask you a question?" I spoke softly as I tucked my hair behind my ear.

"Not if your question is going to lead to a bunch of drama, Viviana. I don't feel like hearing your made-up stories about hearing strange sounds, or being too afraid to stay in here for a few hours by yourself. When I was your age I used to—" I interrupted her.

"It's nothing like that. I was just wondering—" I paused. "I mean...I want you to have a good time and everything, but don't pick up a new boyfriend. I mean, you of course can have a new boyfriend but can you wait for a little while?"

"Wait for a while? Your father has been dead for two years. I have a right to seek romance and happiness free of guilt," she said defensively.

"I know, but..." I paused, making sure to choose my words carefully. "It seems like whenever you get a new boyfriend, you never seem to have time for me." I looked into her eyes and immediately saw sparks of anger.

"How selfish of you, Viviana, I can't believe you just said that to me!" she barked, and I flinched. "Don't you want me to be happy? Don't you want me to fall in love again? I have to work three times as hard to get a guy to notice me because of young girls like you!" She spoke as if some guy had already chosen me over her.

"I'm only thirteen and I don't even like boys," I gently reminded her.

She inhaled deeply and then released a short, quick huff of air. "You may be thirteen but your body has blossomed and looks just as old as mine." I immediately felt self-conscious.

I hugged myself as I leaned my back against the wall near the light switch.

"The only things you're missing are my stretch marks and belly fat. You're prettier than me and if I were to meet a guy, I plan to do everything I can to make sure he stays focused on my sexy body and not yours." My mother stared at me as if I were a direct threat to winning over the man she'd hoped to catch. She moved toward the dresser, grabbed a pack of Pall Mall 100's and tapped out one of the cigarettes. She reached for her lighter, spun the wheel and lit her smoke. She inhaled deeply before expelling a long plume of smoke.

"You're the one who took my sexy body from me. Before I had you I could walk down the street and stop traffic without even trying. These days, that's not so freaking easy." She placed her cigarette in an ashtray and began tugging at the fabric of the dress.

I took a hard swallow and boldly said, "You sound like you hate me."

She chuckled condescendingly. "Hate and envy are closely related, remember that." Salena stepped out of her bedroom and walked across the hall to the bathroom. Before I could ask another question she slammed the door shut, leaving me completely confused as to what I'd done wrong or what she meant. That happened three years ago. A lot has changed since then, most of which has not been for the better.

I was scratching a mosquito bite on my forearm as I stood in front of Our Lady of Guadalupe Church on Chicago's Southeast side. I noticed my skin had turned as red as a strawberry as I waited on my girlfriend Toya Taylor to arrive. An ugly boy, about fifteen with zits galore, walked past, puckered his lips and blew me a kiss. I gave him a repulsive glare as I noticed his ill-fitting black slacks, and the fact that he didn't have on any socks with his white dress shoes.

"Ugh," I mumbled.

The last thing I wanted was an ugly and broke boyfriend. Hell, I had expensive tastes and needed a man who was getting paid. Admittedly, I wasn't dressed in anything spectacular, just my blue jean shorts, a green T-shirt and a pair of worn-out but comfortable pink flip-flops. My black hair was braided into a long ponytail that cascaded down the center of my back, stopping between my shoulder blades. I am tall, slender and have been told countless times that my lips are shaped like Angelina Jolie's. Some days, I actually wished that I was her so I could live her fairy-tale life. I would have looked more fly if I'd had a pair of sexy sunglasses and the designer handbag I'd seen at a store in the mall a few days before. I hated being broke and struggling for everything. If my father were still around he would've made sure I had everything my heart desired, no matter what it cost. He was the best father a girl could ask for. He had his problems and did stuff he wasn't proud of in order to survive, but he did what he had to do out of love, and that counted for a lot in my book. At that moment, while lost in my thoughts, an elderly woman with aged, wrinkled skin, a white head scarf and an advanced case of osteoporosis begged for my attention.

"I have fruit and bottled water. Would you like to buy something?" The frail woman held up a raggedy brown wicker basket. Her cheerless eyes looked as if they'd only

seen depression and disappointment and not a single moment of joy.

"I don't have any money," I answered. She gave me a sor-
rowful frown before shuffling on to some other person. I lost
sight of the old woman in the crowd of people who'd come
from all around the city to watch the Mexican Independence
Day Parade. I heard someone in the crowd shout out above a
wailing police siren, "Viva Mexico!" followed by an equally
enthusiastic chant of "Viva Chicago!" The sound of car horns,
cheers and ringing bells filled the air and signaled the start
of the parade. I moved closer to the street, watching as par-
ticipants walked down the center of the boulevard, swaying
the Mexican flag in one hand and waving to strangers with
the other. A float went by with women and men dressed in
traditional Mexican clothing danced around to folk music
that was blaring out of stereo speakers. I watched with little
interest. I only had a vague idea of what the parade symbol-
ized. I knew it had something to do about a war for independence from Spain.

"There you are! Girl, I've been walking all over the place
looking for you." Toya seemed to appear out of nowhere.
She tugged at my arm to get my attention.

"I've been standing in the same spot. I haven't moved," I
said as I took one last look at a parade float.

"What? You want to go out there and be part of the parade now?" Toya asked mockingly as she folded up a newspaper she was carrying.

"No way." I quickly cleared up her preconceived notion.

"What does all of this mean, anyway?" Toya asked. She
adjusted the backpack that hung on her right shoulder.

"Hell if I know." I shrugged.

"Well, this is the parade for your people. Don't you know anything about it?" Toya pressed the issue.

Becoming irritated, I said, "It's about some war. That's all I know." The cheers from the crowd grew louder and the streets seemed to swell with an even larger number of people.

"Oh, hell no. Hold up, girl," Toya said, glaring down at my feet. "What's up with the flip-flops?"

Glancing down at my feet, I asked, "What's wrong with them?"

"If we need to make a quick move, you can't run in those," Toya pointed out, and then she mocked me by flapping her feet on the ground like a duck.

"I thought you were just going to show me how to do it. I didn't think we were going to actually do something today," I said.

"I knew I should've called you back to find out what you were wearing," Toya griped.

"Well, if it's a problem maybe we should wait until another time," I said sharply.

"Nah, it is what it is now. At least I know you won't pull a Keysha on me," she said.

"Pull a Keysha?" I asked, lowering my eyebrows and slightly frowning.

"Keysha is this girl who used to be my friend. You remind me of her." Toya smirked.

"I remind you of her how?"

"In a lot of ways. Just like you, I took her under my wing and showed her the ropes on how to get paid by jacking people for their stuff. But then she snaked out on me by disappearing when the police caught me."

"Hold up, when all of that go down?"

"Girl, that's a chapter in my past. I didn't stay locked up for long, but when I saw Keysha again, I cut her like this." Toya made a quick jerking motion at my face to show me what she'd done.

"Was she messed up afterward?"

"She was hurt bad enough," Toya proudly boasted.

"What happened to her?" I asked.

"She moved away into a big house with her rich daddy," Toya said as we began walking along the sidewalk. "She has a brother named Mike I used to kick it with."

"Oh, yeah, what happened with that?"

"He was so lame. I tricked him into giving me about three hundred dollars and I stole his car. I sold it to a chop shop for a few thousand dollars."

"See, that's what I'm talking about. I need to get paid like that," I said, longing for money to fulfill my every need.

"Keep hanging with me and I'll show you how to do it," Toya said confidently. "Now you can hang with me all day, right?"

"Yeah, my mother is off somewhere with her boyfriend at a barbecue. She doesn't care about where I am or what I'm doing. Sometimes I wish I had my own apartment so I wouldn't have to deal with her at all. I could make it on my own in a place that doesn't charge much for rent. All I'd need is a crappy job and I'd be all set."

"A job?" Toya laughed. "Girl, me and my baby daddy had our own place for a minute and neither one of us had a job.

The only reason we moved was because some stuff went down. That's why I'm back at my grandmother's house."

"How were you paying for rent?" I asked.

"See, that's why you need to hang with me. I can teach you everything. I can show you how to get over on the system to get everything you want. First, you need to get pregnant so you can get money for your baby. Then all you have to do is keep signing up for assistance programs that help teen mothers pay their rent and buy food for you and the baby. With rent and food taken care of, you're on easy street."

"Really?" I asked, enticed by the possibility of having my own place.

"Yeah, then you can make quick cash on the side doing all kinds of stuff." Toya spoke as if she had it all completely mapped out.

"Wait a minute," I said, rethinking what she'd just said. "Isn't the man supposed to take care of his woman and children?"

"Viviana, that only happens in fairy tales. Come on, now, don't be so naive. Every girl knows that guys are not going to step up when the baby arrives. The quickest way for a girl to lose her man is to start sounding like a nagging wife. You see, that's why I get along so well with my boyfriend. I don't make him do anything that he doesn't want to do. It's sort of like reverse psychology. If I don't cause any drama, he does stuff willingly. If I'm in his face all of the time, then he's going to snap. Get it?"

"Yeah, that makes sense," I agreed.

"See, that's why I love that show called *Sixteen and Pregnant*. Every girl on there does nothing but complain and nearly all of them end up without their boyfriend. If I were on an episode, I'd show them how to be a good mother, keep the baby's father and live on their own."

"It would be so cool if that happened, Toya. I can see you now, just being real with it and telling young girls how to do things the right way," I said excitedly.

"Yeah, then I'd become famous and hang out with celebrities," Toya said, fantasizing about the possibilities.

"Ooo, you know what would happen next, girl?" I stopped walking then turned to face her.

"No. What?" she asked.

"The people from *Dancing with the Stars* would call you," I said, starting to truly believe in the ultimate lifestyle we were fabricating.

"They probably would, girl. I could be like the black version of Bristol Palin. Lord knows that I can dance better than her. Girl, I'd get up there and do the booty clap dance and drive America wild like Beyoncé, Shakira or this old-school chick named Josephine Baker."

"Josephine Baker? Who is that?" I asked, because I'd never heard of her.

"Girl, she was some actress and dancer from like the 1920s or something," Toya explained.

"The 1920s!" I blurted out, surprised she'd mentioned someone who lived so long ago.

"The only reason I know about her is because I was sitting up one night dealing with Junior's cranky behind. Anyway, by the time he went to bed I couldn't sleep so I started watching television. I got caught up watching either the Discovery or History Channel, I can't remember which. Anyway, they showed some old video of this chick Josephine doing the booty clap and I was like, what the hell!"

"Are you serious?" I asked.

"Yeah, and Josephine was killing it! She was like a beast with it," Toya tried to imitate what she'd seen and I cracked up laughing.

"Oh, no you didn't just move like that out here in front of all these people." I continued to laugh in an effort to make her feel self-conscious.

"Whatever!" Toya fired back, waving off my snide remark.

"So look here, Miss Flip-flop-clippity-clop," Toya said, making a joke about my shoes. "I'm going to teach you how you can spot someone whose pocket you can easily pick. Are you ready for your lesson?"

"Yeah," I answered, feeling a rush of adrenaline race through me.

"Okay, there are several ways this works. For beginners like you, crowded areas like this parade are better because people will not be suspicious if you get very close to them. If you were to walk up behind them, and ask if they could move over a little so you can see, it's not a big deal. That's when you use that opportunity to bump them and find out where their wallet, sunglasses, car keys or cell phone is located. Once you've located what you want, you have to time the next bump against them and move quickly. You need to have quick hands but they need be gentle at the same time."

"But won't they feel me taking their stuff?" I asked, thinking that I'd notice if someone had ripped me off.

"No, most times people have no clue. Plus, you have to find the right target," Toya said, looking around. "See that

guy over there with his sunglasses in his shirt pocket?" Toya
pointed the guy out.

"Yeah, I see him," I answered.

"I'm going to go get those sunglasses. Stay here and just
watch," she said. I watched Toya snake her way through the
crowded sidewalk, moving purposefully toward the man with
the sunglasses. When she got close enough she pretended
to stumble into him. She braced herself against his chest as
he tried to keep her from falling over. Once Toya gathered
herself she said thank-you and moved on. I watched as Toya
disappeared and then turned my attention back to the man,
noticing his sunglasses were gone.

"Damn, she's good," I mumbled to myself. I stood there
for about ten minutes wondering where Toya had gone. Before long, she came up behind me and when I was looking in
the other direction she said, "Boo!" The sound of her voice
startled me.

"Toya, what's wrong with you?" I said, turning my full
attention to her.

"I just wanted to show you just how close I can get to
you without you knowing it. Come on, let's walk this way."
Toya and I maneuvered away from the crowd and down a
side street where there were less people. Once she felt safe
she opened up the newspaper she'd been carrying.

"See, I have his sunglasses and a twenty-dollar bill that he
had tucked in that pocket." I was so excited that I wanted to
scream but I held myself in check. I was ready to try it because I'd hoped to get some money, as well.

"Where did you learn how to do this?" I asked.

"Does it really matter?" Toya answered my question with one of her own.

"Well, I suppose not," I responded, feeling silly for asking.

"Look. I'm taking the time to show you how to get paid, not to give you a history lesson on where I picked up this skill. Now that I have twenty dollars in my pocket, I'm hungry for some more cash and prizes. With a crowd of this size I can easily rack up two thousand dollars' worth of money and merchandise that can be sold."

"Are you serious?" I whispered.

"Totally. Question is, are you game? Do you want to make some money today?" she asked.

"You know I do." I didn't hesitate to answer.

"Okay, then here is what we're going to do. Since you're wearing those damn flip-flops and can't move the way I need you to, you're going to be my dump-off person. I'm going to walk through the crowd and find targets and get merchandise. Once I have something, I'm going to walk back past you and hand whatever I get to you. Do not look at it. Just drop it in the backpack quickly. Every time I drop something off to you, I want you to walk down one block and wait. I'll find you. We're going to work this side of the street and then cross over and work the other side. You got it?"

"Yeah, I can handle that," I said confidently.

"If someone tries to rob you, all I know is you'd better fight." Toya was very clear on that point.

"What about the police? What if they catch you?" I asked.

"Catch me with what? I'm dropping stuff back off to you.

You're the one holding the backpack of stolen merchandise, not me. Do you have a problem with that?"

"Hell no!" I wasn't afraid of anything.

"Good. When I'm done we'll head back to my place and see what I've pulled in." Toya met my gaze, searching my eyes once more to see if I had the nerves for this.

"I got this," I reassured her.

Nodding her head approvingly, Toya said, "Cool." As she walked away I began to think about my mother, my current living arrangements and how I'd met Toya.

My mother and I had been staying with my grandmother Esmeralda for two weeks straight, because once again we were homeless. Then one day out of the clear blue my mother walked into the house in high spirits, talking about how she fell in love in one night. I felt my stomach turn when she made her grand announcement. A few days later all of our belongings were once again packed up and we moved to the Southside of Chicago to some apartment building on Martin Luther King Jr. Drive. Her new man, a dude named Martin, was heavily involved with some huge motorcycle club. Martin had a baritone voice, tattoos covering a good portion of his body, and a really quick temper. Once again, my mother had selected a loser she'd hoped to turn into her prince.

When I first met Martin I had a difficult time looking at him because his left eye kept drifting, which somehow made me feel as if I were going cross-eyed. Martin loved his motorcycle brothers and bragged continually about the brawls he'd been involved in. Personally, I thought he was a little too old to be getting into fights, but apparently for him it was not a big deal.

"I'll lay my life on the line and take a bullet for any one of my brothers." That was another thing about Martin. He sounded as if he didn't have the sense that God gave a rock. He was from the South and mumbled when he spoke.

"I'll take a bullet for your mom, too, because she is such a sweet woman." He raked his fingers through his chin whiskers, which were long enough to be coiled into dreadlocks. My mother, who was sitting on his lap at the time, giggled like a sixth grader experiencing her first kiss behind the school building. Listening to him and watching her gush over his every word was truly disgusting.

Martin's two-bedroom apartment was the ultimate sleazy bachelor pad. Every lamp was shaped like a motorcycle. He believed road signs from the highway made excellent wall art, and the room I had to sleep in was more than musty. It smelled like butt farts that didn't have the good sense to evaporate.

"This is the room where any one of the boys can come and crash if they need to for any reason. You should consider yourself lucky to have such a room," Martin said as he placed my belongings on an old mattress that squeaked from the slightest pressure.

"I know it doesn't have the look or feel of a girl's room, but hey, I'm sure you'll make the best of it," he said. Just as he was about to leave he spotted something on the floor behind the closet door. I glanced at a naked lady on the magazine cover that he went to pick up.

"Sorry about that. One of the boys must've been in a jam and…um…"

"It's okay," I said, moving away from him.

"I'll go and get your mom for you," he said as he exited the room.

"Oh, my God! I can't wait to leave this place. I can't believe my mother moved us in with this guy," I mumbled. Standing in the center of the bedroom I began scratching my skin, which suddenly felt dirty. I grabbed my belongings off the bed and placed them in the closet. That's when I spotted a fishing knife on the floor next to a pair of black motorcycle boots. I picked the knife up and pulled open the blade, which was about eight inches long.

"Perfect," I whispered. "I'm going to sleep with this, just in case Martin gets confused as to which bed he's supposed to be sleeping in."

On the third evening of our stay with Martin, he came home screaming like a madman about some deal he and the brotherhood had made that fell through. I exited my bedroom and walked up behind Martin, who was standing by the kitchen table situated near the back door. He reeked of alcohol, cigar smoke and body funk. Then for no apparent reason whatsoever he turned his anger on my mom. He began screaming at her as she was scraping leftover Chinese food out of its white container onto a plate to warm up for him. I guess she figured the best way to calm him down was to feed him.

"I don't want any damn Chinese food. I want some Southern cooking. Make me some neck bones, lima beans and corn bread," he yelled at her.

Martin's request for soul food presented two big problems. There was no food in the refrigerator and, second, my mom was a Mexican woman who didn't grow up in the South on Southern soul food. He moved closer to her and appeared as if he wanted to beat her. I removed the fishing knife from my pocket and extended the blade to its full length. If Martin placed a hand on her I'd planned to stab him in the back and tell my mother that it was time to go.

"Viviana." My mom got my attention. "Wait outside for a minute."

"What? Are you serious? He looks like he wants to choke you to death and you want me to leave?"

"You heard your mama, little girl, now get on out of here." Martin turned and looked at me. With boldness and confidence I held up the knife. The one thing my daddy taught me was how to protect myself.

"What are you going to do with that besides tick me off?" Martin's voice was filled with threats.

"If you hit my mother or me you'll find out," I answered him.

"Viviana, go outside. It will be okay." My mother once again tried to get me to leave. "Come on, it's okay." She approached me and walked me to the front door. "Just sit outside for a minute. It's a nice day. Even better, go for a walk at the park. When you come back everything will be fine, and put that knife away."

"But he's…"

"Viviana, go!" My mother opened the door. I had no choice but to leave. I went outside and sat on the steps in front of the building. I was so irritated. I wanted to leave but I didn't have a dime to my name. I would have called one of my girlfriends but my cell phone was out of minutes. My mother was supposed to get money from Martin to pay for it, but it didn't look like that was going to happen anytime soon. Feeling miserable, I buried my face in my hands and closed my eyes. Not long after that, this girl appeared with a little boy who was just learning how to walk upstairs. I moved out of her way.

"What's up?" she greeted me. I shrugged my shoulders.

"You're the new girl from apartment 407, right?" she asked.

"Yeah, how did you know that?" I asked.

"I know everything that goes on in this building. My name is Toya. Toya Taylor." She extended her hand.

"I'm Viviana Vargas." I reached over and shook her hand.

"Are you okay? Because you look like you could use a friend," Toya said.

"I've seen better days," I admitted. Her son placed his tiny hand on my knee. "Your son is handsome."

"He's more like a handful, if you ask me." Toya chuckled.

"What's his name?"

"Junior," she answered.

"Why are you just sitting out here on these dirty steps?" Toya asked the obvious question. I shook my head and just started venting about everything. Before I could stop myself I realized that I'd shared way too much with someone I didn't know at all.

"You know what? I've seen days like that," she said sympathetically.

"Really?" I asked, not fully believing her.

"Of course I have and I know what it feels like." I didn't

say anything and Toya didn't continue on her way. The silence between us became awkward.

"Listen, why don't you come up to my apartment? You can sit around and watch videos on VH1 with me," Toya offered.

"You don't even know me and you're willing to invite me into your house?" I glanced over at her to see if she'd lost her mind.

"You don't look like the type who'd kill someone." Toya smirked. I reached into my pocket and pulled out my knife. I wanted to prove to her that she really didn't know me or understand what I'd do if I were backed into a corner.

Toya smiled, seemingly pleased with the fact that I was carrying a weapon.

"This is my protection against any fool who tries to hurt me or my mother. Especially that fool she's upstairs with now." I glanced up at Martin's apartment window. I was still worried about my mother.

"My girl. I can tell that you and I are going to get along well. Come inside with me—I won't bite, I promise." I don't know what made me go with her. Perhaps it was a combination of boredom and frustration but I was glad that I did.

# three

*MAYA*

MY leg had completely healed up and I no longer needed to wear my hideous-looking orthopedic boot. Going to physical therapy was a real drag, but the therapist said she was impressed with how quickly I was recovering from my injury. In many ways I felt rather invincible, like no real harm could ever happen to me. From time to time my ankle would feel very stiff and would swell if I did too much walking. Whenever that would happen I'd just place an ice pack on it until the swelling subsided.

I'd tried to schedule a romantic time with Misalo at my house when I was still limping around with the orthopedic boot. But that didn't happen because Misalo had forgotten that he had to go to his summer soccer training camp, and right after that his family flew to San Diego, California, for a family reunion. I was so frustrated because I hadn't seen him in a long time and the last thing I wanted was for him to be on the other side of the country. With Misalo being so far away I was absolutely miserable. At night I'd pull out my iPod and listen to love songs because I missed him so much—I missed his laugh, his cute face and all of the attention he showered me with. There were so many things that I wanted to do with him and even more things that I wanted to do to him. I'd never felt the way I did about Misalo with anyone else and I certainly couldn't imagine myself being with another guy. I actually told him that one night when we were having a late-night phone conversation. I was being extra careful to make sure the walls didn't carry my voice throughout the house.

"I have something to tell you, but you can't turn around and say the same thing back to me," I explained as I got more relaxed underneath my covers and pressed the phone even closer to my ear.

"What is it?" Misalo whispered. He had such a smooth and romantic voice. I don't know if it's possible to fall in love with the sound of someone's voice, but I most certainly was in love with his. I could just listen to him talk to me forever.

I closed my eyes and gently whispered, "I never want to be with anyone else."

"Neither do I," he responded.

"You can't say the same thing that I just said to you. It cheapens the moment," I griped, wishing he could take his words back.

"But it's true, Maya. I am so into you. It's like I'm drawn to you in a way that I just can't explain."

After he said that to me I immediately forgave him. Just hearing how much he cared for me made my heart soar on the promises of true love. "Remember when we first met?" I asked, wishing he was near me so I could snuggle up in his warm embrace and inhale his scent.

Misalo chuckled. "Of course I do. It was during a school pep assembly for the homecoming football game. I was sitting on the bleachers directly in front of you and you began screaming like a psychopath when the band played the school spirit song. You were so loud that I swore you exploded my eardrum. Besides, I think you were the only one in the entire school who knew the words."

"I did not scream that loudly," I remarked playfully.

"Oh, yes you did." He laughed.

"Whatever!" I forgot why I'd even asked him the question.

"I remember holding my hand to my ear and turning to look at you. I was about to say something foul until our eyes met. I couldn't stop looking at you."

"I know. You gave me a complex. I thought I had a booger or something dangling out of my nostril." I giggled at the memory.

"At that moment I remember thinking I had to know everything about you. I didn't care about the roaring crowd, or whether or not our team won or who was looking. Time seemed to stop for a moment. You were like an angel."

I released a long sigh and then said, "It took me a moment to realize what the look you were giving me was for, but when I did, I felt the same way. Everything just seemed to stop. I remember thinking that I wanted to kiss you, but I didn't even know you."

"I would've let you kiss me. Hell, I would've given you my virginity at that moment, had you asked for it," Misalo confessed.

"Well, I would not have given you mine. Your eyes were

pretty, but they didn't have the power to make me want to do all of that."

"Well, your eyes had that type of impact on me. It was truly love at first sight."

"So, tell me how much you love me now?" I wanted to know if his heart was just as lovesick as mine.

"I love you so much that if you asked me for the moon, I'd snatch it from the stars and give it you." Misalo's words were like a tender melody to my ears. My heart melted like ice cream sitting on a hot stove. "Really?" I wanted to hear him say it to me once again.

"Yes, really. I wish I could hold you right now, Maya. I wish I could look into your eyes and see your soul, which I know shines brighter than moonlight. I wish we could be someplace right now enjoying each other."

I released a long exhale. "Oh, Misalo, I love you so much," I said, surrendering all of my feelings to the moment. "I wish there was something I could do to bring us closer right now."

"I have an idea," Misalo said. "But before you give me a quick no, think about it and then give me a slow yes."

"What do you have in mind?" I asked suspiciously thinking that perhaps he wanted me to talk like a nasty girl from one of those 1-900 numbers.

"Okay, you know I'd do anything to make sure that I always stay on your mind, right?" Misalo spoke confidently.

"Of course I do," I whispered as I twisted a strand of my hair.

"I want you to text me a picture of yourself," Misalo said.

"I'm in the bed and my hair is a mess. Besides, I don't have on any decent clothes. I'm not trying to scare you away, baby." I couldn't believe he wanted to see me when I wasn't looking my best.

"You're not catching my drift, Maya," Misalo said in a smooth and calm voice.

"What do you mean?" I asked.

"Text me a naked picture."

I didn't think I'd heard him right, so I sat up and repositioned myself before turning up the volume on my phone. "What did you just ask me to do?"

"Come on, don't be like that. Be a fun girlfriend and text me a sexy photo of yourself so that I can look at you."

I was silent for a long moment as I processed what he was requesting. "No way."

"Why not?"

"Because, what if the photo gets lost or something?" I said, trying to find a rational reason to deny him.

"It's not going to get lost."

"Well, I don't want a naked photo of me floating around."

"Maya, I just want to look at you. Then I'll delete it. I promise," Misalo pleaded, his voice sounded genuine and assuring.

"Send me one of you and then I'll think about it," I suggested, thinking he'd be too shy or embarrassed to actually do it.

"I don't have a problem with it because I love you and I'll do anything to make sure that I stay on your mind. Come on, Maya, just this one time." Misalo was making me feel both guilty and obligated to fulfill his little fantasy. I didn't know what to do or say, so I remained quiet.

"Forget it. I'll talk to you later." I could hear the frustration and disappointment in his voice.

"Wait a minute. How can you just cut me off like that?" I asked, wanting him to remain on the line.

"You're not going to do it for me. I know you're not. People do it all the time and it's no big deal. It's not like I'm asking you to make it your profile photo on Facebook. You make it sound as if I'm asking you to put on a pair of thong panties and record yourself doing some kind of stripper dance for all of the lurkers and perverts on YouTube. This would be something between two people who love each other. No one will know except us." Misalo really made me feel bad for denying him.

"What do you want to see?" I asked, dreading the response he was going to give.

"Everything. Just go stand naked in front of a mirror, take the photo and send it to me. I'll look at it and then delete it."

"You promise you're going to delete it, *right?*"

"Trust me, Maya. I will. I just need this. I need to see you." Misalo begged for me to provide him with the freakiness he desired.

"Fine." I reluctantly agreed to do it.

"Great, I'm waiting for it." Misalo's voice once again sounded cheery and that made me even more uneasy.

"I'll do it tomorrow," I said, suddenly getting cold feet.

"No. I want it right now!" he snapped.

"I look crazy right now, Misalo." I hoped he'd hear how emotionally conflicted I was about doing it.

"I don't care. We're going to always be together and sooner or later I'm going to see exactly what you look like when you're asleep and when you first wake up. I don't care how your hair looks. Just do it, Maya."

I sighed, then reluctantly surrendered to his will. "Okay. I'll go do it now."

"Cool. No one will ever see the pictures, I promise," he said.

"Okay, I'll call you back once I've taken them and sent them to you. I want to make sure that only you receive the pictures."

"I'll be waiting," he said and hung up.

I exhaled as I got out of bed and turned on my bedroom light. There was a full-length mirror on the back of my bedroom door. I stood in front of it and thought to myself, *Maya, he loves you. He's not like other boys and it's the least you can do for the guy who saved your life.* I studied my reflection and I truly did not look attractive. I didn't have on any makeup, my hair wasn't styled and I certainly looked as if I'd just awoken. I went to the bathroom, and freshened up. When I came back to my room I shut the door and once again looked at myself in the mirror. Just as I was about to take off my pajamas and send him a nude photo I came up with a brilliant idea. My mom and I had recently been shopping. I'd purchased numerous pairs of matching bra-and-panty sets. Since pink was my favorite color, I decided that I was much more comfortable sending him provocative photos of myself in underwear. In my mind the photos would be revealing enough.

With those thoughts in my head, I took a number of playful photos. A kissy-face shot, the innocent girl shot, the who-you-looking-at shot, and another one looking over my shoulder and showing my tush. The final photo was of me straddling the chair with some black high-heeled shoes on. All of the photos were tricky to get because I was using the full-length mirror to capture my reflection. However, I thought the photos I sent were fun and flirtatious.

The moment directly after I forwarded the final picture, panicky butterflies began prancing around in the pit of my belly. Feeling paranoid, I immediately called Misalo to make sure that he got them.

"Hello," he answered his phone.

"Did you get them?" I asked fretfully.

"Them? You sent more than one?" He seemed pleased.

"Yes, I sent several," I said as I started gnawing on my fingernails.

"No, nothing has come through yet."

"Oh, no!" I freaked out, thinking that in my hastiness I had forwarded the pictures to someone else. Just as I was about to take a look at my sent file I heard Misalo say, "Hang on, something just came through." There was a brief period of silence before I heard him say. "You're not naked."

"No, but I'm close enough to being naked," I said defensively. "What, you don't like them?"

"No, they're cool. I feel like I'm looking at an underwear model though." Misalo chuckled.

"That was the idea," I said, feeling very self-conscious. "Don't you like the color of my underwear? You know pink is my favorite color."

"I wasn't paying attention to the color of your underwear. I'm more focused on your hot body," he admitted.

"Okay, now you're starting to sound sort of like a pervert. Is this what I have to look forward to when we get old together? Are you going to become a dirty old man who likes looking at magazines filled with women modeling underwear?" I asked because I really did want to know.

"Who knows what I'll be like as an old man, but one thing is for sure. I'll never get tired of looking at you." Misalo made a kissing sound. My heart sort of melted at that point.

"Oh, I really like this over-the-shoulder shot. You have sweet-looking buns." He giggled.

"Okay, time to delete those photos, just as you promised." I reminded him of his promise to me.

"You have an awesome body, Maya," Misalo said as he continued to ogle my photos.

"Hello! Delete them, Misalo!" I said with more authority.

"Okay, hang on." Misalo remained quiet for a second before speaking again. "Okay, I've deleted the photos."

"Are you sure?" I asked suspiciously.

"Yes, Maya. The photos are gone," he assured me.

"Good!" I exhaled.

"I love you," Misalo said sweetly.

I smiled and whispered back, "I love you, too."

If it had not been for Keysha, I'm positive I would have totally lost my marbles from longing so much for Misalo. She finally convinced me to get out of the house and do something other than sit around staring out my bedroom window as if I were Bella from the *Twilight* story, waiting for Edward Cullen to return. Keysha said it was time for us to have a girls' day out so that we could really catch up on everything that had been going on, as well as do some shopping. I tried to get out of it by reminding her that I was unemployed and had no money. She said money wasn't a problem because she'd just cashed her paycheck. That was the great thing about having a BFF like Keysha. She was so giving. If I saw something I liked but didn't have the cash for it, she'd buy it for me and I'd pay her back whenever I could. So, on a Sunday afternoon, after getting permission from my parents, I found myself standing at the corner of State and Randolph Streets with Keysha. We'd just exited one department store and decided to head south toward Old Navy.

"I can't believe you're thinking about dating Wesley again," I said as I removed my sunglasses from my purse and put them on.

"I didn't say that I was going to date him again, I just said we've been talking." Keysha opened her purse and removed some chewing gum. "You want some?" She offered me a piece.

"Yeah," I said, taking a stick.

"Now that he's gone through detox he sounds like the Wesley that swept me off of my feet, and it's sort of nice."

"Even after the way he played you with Lori? I'm just shocked to hear that you're still willing to give him the time of day," I said, trying to understand why she'd want to go back to him.

"Lori is still around. I saw her at the grocery store the other night. She flipped up her middle finger at me and I was like, whatever, chick!" Keysha laughed.

"Well, isn't she going to be a problem if you and Wesley hook up again?" I asked.

"I'm not worried about Lori at all. She knows that if she

even dreams about beating me up she'd better wake up, call me and apologize," Keysha said, laughing.

"Okay, but you know Lori is a drama queen," I reminded her.

"A drama queen who has burned two guys. She's so nasty!" Keysha said with revulsion.

"Oh, yeah, I forgot that she burned Wesley and Antonio and then Antonio turned around and slept with Priscilla and burned her. What a freaking mess."

"That's Lori for you. One messy girl."

"What about Antonio and Priscilla? Have you heard anything more? Is he going to step up and be a real father?" I asked as I glanced at a pair of shoes in a display window. "Wait a minute. I want to look at these shoes." Keysha stopped and admired the shoes with me.

"I saw Priscilla at the pool the other day. She's eating everything like a cow out on a prairie. She seems to think that her nose has gotten wider and her feet are growing. I'd never heard of such a thing. Anyway, she sat and talked to me for a long time. She said that she's going to have to attend an alternative school for girls in her situation. You know, being a teen mother and all. Apparently, there is some high school that will babysit for her while she takes her classes. But she said she has learned that the school is filled with girls who like to gang bang. So she's really nervous about how she's going to fit in, since she hasn't done anything remotely close to breaking the law."

"Man, that is so jacked up. I would just die if I had to go through something like that," I admitted.

"You and I both," Keysha said, readjusting her purse strap

onto her shoulder. "Priscilla claims that Antonio's parents are very upset about the pregnancy and said that he shouldn't do anything until the baby is born and blood test results confirm that the child actually belongs to him."

"Are you serious? I thought Antonio already owned up to being the father?" I asked.

"He has, but apparently that wasn't good enough for his folks. Priscilla said that his parents are trying to say that she was a promiscuous girl who probably slept with a bunch of guys," Keysha explained.

"Why would his parents think that?" I wondered.

"Priscilla would like to know that as well, but she said that her main focus right now was on having a healthy baby and she didn't have time to deal with a lot of crap."

"She must be miserable," I said, thinking of how she must be feeling.

"That's putting it mildly, although she is hopeful that once the baby arrives all of the doubt will go away and the child will bring everyone together."

"True, that could happen—you just never know," I said, hoping for the best.

"What about Jerry? Have you forgiven him?" I asked.

"Oh, I can't stand that bastard." Keysha looked over at me and I could see the flames of disgust still in her eyes. Jerry was Keysha's most recent ex-boyfriend who didn't care about anything or anyone but himself.

"How is your leg holding up?" Keysha asked as we stepped away from the window and continued on.

"It's fine, just a little achy, but not bad. Since I've been back on my feet I've had to reestablish my position as the oldest child." I laughed.

"Oh, I know that laugh. You've done something," Keysha teased.

"I only did what every older sister in the world has done to her little sister at one point or another." I laughed sinisterly once again.

"What did you do to Anna?" Keysha giggled a little as she leaned in closer to hear what I had to say.

"I beat her down," I answered with great pride.

"What for? What did she do this time?"

"I beat her down for old and new. The entire time my leg was in the cast she purposely did stuff to annoy me."

"I do remember you telling me that you guys were fighting more than usual."

"It doesn't take much for Anna and I to get into it. We still fight over who has the right to control the television," I said as we walked through the doors of Old Navy.

"I know how that is because my brother, Mike, and I go at it all of the time. I swear, if that boy leaves the toilet seat up one more time, I'm going to drown him in toilet water."

"Eww!" I said.

"I'm serious. I think he does stuff like that on purpose," Keysha complained.

"Anna is the same way. The girl knows that I don't like her in my bedroom, yet I keep catching her in my things. Like the other day. I really got ticked off when I noticed that she had a pair of my earrings on. I hate it when she goes on a scavenger hunt through my jewelry."

"I'm glad I don't have a little sister, but I'm not sure having a pea-brained brother is any better," Keysha said as we made our way over to a clearance rack.

"It's not, but thankfully my little brother doesn't annoy me the way Anna does. Speaking of brothers, is Mike still dating Sabrina?" I asked.

"Yeah. I keep telling her that she can do so much better than Mike, but for some odd reason the girl worships the ground that fool walks on. The other day he told me, 'Don't hate the player, hate the game.' I was like, Fool, you don't have any game."

I cracked up laughing as I pulled a cute button-down top off the rack. "Do you think Misalo would like me in something like this?" I held it up for Keysha to see.

"That's cute but I don't think Misalo would notice," she said.

"Of course he would. Misalo is not like other guys, Keysha. He is so into me and notices everything about me," I stated firmly.

"Well, I'm glad one of us has found true romance because Lord knows that I'm no good at it. What's your secret, Maya? How do you keep Misalo happy?" Keysha's question caused me to pause and think.

"I believe that Misalo and I were just made for each other. I think fate brought us together and our love, respect and trust will never be broken."

"That is so sweet," Keysha said, smiling at me. "Do you want that top?"

I looked at the article of clothing again and shook my head no before replacing the top on the rack. "Don't worry, Keysha, I'm sure your Prince Charming will come along."

"As long as he doesn't come with an alcohol problem, an overinflated ego or a baby mama, I'll welcome him with open arms," Keysha said, making fun of all of her past relationships that had gone bad.

"I wish Misalo had a twin brother who could fall in love with you and treat you right," I said.

"I'm cool, girl. Right now I don't have a lot of drama in my life and I'm fine with that." Keysha picked up a blue jean skirt from the same rack as where I'd picked up my top.

"Can I ask a personal question?"

"You know you can ask me anything, Maya." Keysha assured me.

"You ever hear anything from your mother or your grandmother Rubylee?"

Keysha looked over at me. "Why would you ask that question?"

"I don't know. It's just a question," I said, wanting to ease any fears that I was attempting to offend or upset her.

"I actually got a letter from my grandmother Rubylee but I haven't read it yet. As far as my mom goes, I have no clue where she is and as far as I'm concerned she can stay gone."

"And how are you getting along with Jordan and Barbara?" I asked about her dad and her stepmom.

"Good. As long as I don't get into any more trouble, not that I'm looking for any, mind you," Keysha said with a smile.

"I know that's right because, Keysha, you have most certainly had to deal with a lot of drama."

"I'm hungry. Do you want to get something to eat?" Keysha asked.

"Yes, I'm starving." I laughed as Keysha and I placed the clothes we had in our hands back on the rack.

"We could catch the shuttle bus over to Navy Pier and get something to eat at the food court that's over there," Keysha suggested.

"Sounds like a plan to me," I said as we exited the store. "Besides, maybe we'll run into a really hot guy who's perfect for you."

# four

## VIVIANA

After the parade, Toya and I came back to the apartment where she lived with her elderly and blind grandmother. We went into her bedroom and emptied the backpack on top of her mattress. Since there was no chair in the room I sat on her bed, which squeaked loudly like birds arguing over a worm after a morning rain shower. The pack was filled with all types of merchandise. Cash, wallets, credit cards, cellular phones and watches. I was absolutely amazed by all of the stuff Toya was able to take from people without them realizing it. She definitely had a skill that I wanted to learn.

"You didn't pocket any of the cash I gave you to hold, did you?" Toya asked while eyeing me suspiciously.

"No, why would I do a thing like that?" I answered, offended by her accusation.

"It's not that I don't really trust you, Viviana, it's just that you may think about getting over on me." Toya opened the drawer of a nearby desk. I watched as she pulled out what I thought was a flashlight and aimed it at me. In her hand she held the black object which was slightly larger than a digital camera.

"What's that, a flashlight?" I asked.

"Yeah, it can be used as that, too," Toya said as she turned on the light.

"What do you need a flashlight for?"

"This little thing here is more than a flashlight." Toya flicked another switch on the device. It was then I heard the eerie crackling of an electric current.

Horrified, I asked, "What are you doing?"

"Making sure that we have a clear understanding," Toya said, pressing the trigger on the device again, causing it to make another gruesome sound.

"A clear understanding about what?" I immediately rose to my feet, grabbed a pillow and backed away from her.

"When it comes to my money I don't trust anyone, not even my blind grandmother." Toya once again pulled the trigger on what I now realized was a stun gun. The sound echoed in the room like wood crackling in a fireplace.

"So you're going to stun me?" I bravely stood my ground and prepared for our friendship to suddenly turn sour. I wasn't about to turn and run away from her. My father taught me to never run away from a fight.

"Where did you get that?" I asked, positioning myself just out of the reach of her arm.

"This is Chicago. You can get anything you want on the streets for the right price." Toya extended her arm toward me and once again pressed the trigger. "This baby carries a charge of two million volts and can—" Before she could finish her sentence, I stepped forward and slung the pillow as hard as I could at her hand that held the stun gun. Toya's arm jerked away from her body. With my left hand I grabbed her wrist, planted my right leg behind her left one, and in one quick move swept one of her legs from beneath her.

"What the hell!" Toya cried out as she reached for my hair. I quickly jerked away so that she couldn't pull it.

Toya easily went to the ground. I stepped on her wrist with my left foot, breaking her hold on the stun gun, and then dropped my right knee into her chest, knocking the breath out of her lungs. Gasping for air, Toya gave up easily.

"If you're going to zap me, then do it, don't waste time talking." I stepped on Toya's wrist a little harder. Her hand opened up and I took the weapon. Toya rolled over onto her side and started coughing. I glanced down at her, feeling very little pity. I pulled the trigger on the stun gun, and thought about zapping her with it and taking everything on the bed. I was just about to do it when I felt a little arm wrap around my leg. I looked down and Toya's son was balancing himself against my leg while sucking a blue pacifier.

"Toya, I know you're in there. I heard you tumbling around. Did you trip or something? You need to take Junior. You know I can't watch him for you now that he's starting to crawl and walk." I looked over my shoulder and saw Toya's grandmother. She had on black glasses, a one-size-fits-all flower-print dress draped over her round body, and a pair of brown house slippers. She stood as still as a tree, with a broom in her hand, ready to use it as a weapon if need be. "Toya, are you okay? I heard you come in here with someone. Did that boy hit you again? How many times are you going to let him beat up on you before you realize he doesn't love you?" I don't know what happened to me in that moment. Maybe it was the fact that Toya's blind grandmother was so concerned, or the fact that Toya's boyfriend was beating her, something that I personally would not have put up with. I just know that for reasons I don't fully understand, I felt a little sympathy for her.

"Toya's okay," I answered.

"Who are you?" Her grandmother looked in the direction of my voice. I put the stun gun down and helped Toya to her feet. She jerked her arm away from me as she massaged the spot where I'd planted my knee.

"I'm Viviana, from upstairs," I answered.

"Oh, well, where is Toya? Did she leave you in here by yourself?" she asked, anxiety etched across her features.

"No, Grandma." Toya finally spoke.

"Well, why didn't you say something? I've told you about playing around like that with me. You know I only have one good nerve left," her grandmother scolded.

"I know," Toya answered. "I'm sorry, I wasn't paying attention when you walked in. I have Junior." Toya picked up her son and perched him on her left hip. She moved toward the doorway, took her grandmother's hand and said, "Come on, tell me what show you want to listen to and I'll turn the television to that channel."

When Toya returned to the room a few minutes later, I'd once again picked up the stun gun and was toying around with it. She stood in the doorway and cleared her throat. I looked over at her and she still had her son perched on her hip.

"Your move. What now?" Toya asked, apparently humbled

by the fact I'd rendered her completely helpless. I pressed the trigger on the stun gun again and then approached her. She took a deep breath, perhaps fearing that I was going to jolt her.

"You're one twisted chick. Do you know that?" Toya looked me directly in the eyes but said nothing. "You need to use this on your boyfriend and not me," I said as I turned the stun gun off, then handed it back to her.

"I'll let myself out," I said as I started to move past her.

"I wasn't going to zap you, Viviana. I was just playing around. You didn't have to jump me like that," Toya griped.

"What do you mean, you weren't going to do it?" I glared at her, confused by what she was saying.

"I wasn't going to electrocute you. I only wanted to scare you into giving me any money that you may have taken," Toya confessed as she walked back into the room. She opened up a closet door and removed a foldaway playpen for Junior. I went over and helped her set it up.

"Obviously, you didn't take any of the cash. Other people I've worked with have always taken a little something for themselves. Whenever I pull out the stun gun and pull the trigger a few times, I get the money that they've taken from me." Toya placed her son safely inside the playpen, then walked back over to her bed and sat down. "So, why didn't you take any of the money?"

I shrugged and said, "The thought never crossed my mind. I'm sorry that you didn't trust me." I glanced down at my watch to see what time it was. "It's getting late." I turned and made my way toward the front door. As soon as I pulled it open, Toya's palm landed flat against it and slammed it back shut. I looked at her.

"I'm sorry. I've always had a hard time making friends. I've been through a lot of stuff, okay? And the minute I feel like someone is trying to take advantage of me or disrespect me I have to handle my business. Do you understand what I'm saying?"

I took a step back and chuckled. "Well, you'd better learn how to fight better than you just did in there."

Toya sighed. "You caught me totally off guard. You fight like a guy. Where did you learn how to move like that?"

"My dad. He taught me a lot of stuff when I was younger," I answered.

"Where is he now?" Toya asked, touching my shoulder.

"I don't want to talk about it," I immediately replied.

"Okay," Toya said, easily dropping the subject. She handed me one of the cell phones she'd lifted and asked me to hold it. I looked at it for a moment and was about to flip it open with my other hand, but Toya held on to my wrist and asked me a question.

"Do you think you can figure out the pass code to the phone?" she asked, directing my attention back to the phone.

I looked at it again and said, "I don't know."

"That's okay. We don't need to figure out the pass code in order to sell it. Let me have it back." I handed the phone back and Toya draped her arm over my shoulder. "Do you think you can teach me some of those moves though?" she asked with pleading eyes.

I paused in thought for a moment and then smirked. "I

can show you some stuff, but it's not like I'm some kind of martial arts expert."

"I don't care. You know enough. I want you to teach me how to avoid getting all of my hair pulled out." Toya looked in admiration at my hair and touched it briefly.

"I need to get it cut. I have a ton of split ends," I said, running my fingers through it.

Toya took my hand into her own and began walking backward, tugging me along to come back to her room with her.

"Are you sure that we're cool?" I asked her suspiciously.

"Yeah, I won't mess with you unless I plan to really throw down." Toya smiled. "I need someone like you. You can hold your own. Question is, can you keep your mouth shut if you get caught?"

"I'm not like that. I don't snitch," I proudly said.

"Okay. I believe you. Now, let's just put this incident behind us. The Puerto Rican Day Parade is coming up. There is a lot you have to learn in a short period of time." I walked back into Toya's room and sat down on the bed again. I looked at all of the stuff piled up there and asked, "What are you going to do with all of these cell phones?"

"Sell them to shady pawn shops and crooked small-business owners who run cheap cell phone stores."

"How much will you get for all of this stuff?" I asked.

"It depends on the condition they're in and how recent the model is. Sometimes I lift phones that are more than five years old that don't work well. Those phones I sell to this guy who strips them down for the gold, silver and platinum that's in them. He somehow recycles it, but I'm not exactly sure of how he does it. If they're new, like those two iPhones over there, I can get as much as two hundred dollars for them on the street."

"Who is going to pay you that type of money?" I asked curiously.

"Come on, Viviana, I know you're not that naive." Toya looked at me condescendingly.

"I take it that people on the street place orders with you."

"You got it." She picked up the cash and started counting it.

"How much do you have?" I asked once she was done.

"Nine hundred," she said, pleased with the amount she'd gotten for her hard work.

"Man, I could do a few things with that type of money in my pocket," I said, feeling a sense of greed come over me.

"Speaking of pockets, is this yours?" Toya held up a watch that belonged to me. I looked at my arm and, sure enough, she'd swiped it without my knowing it.

"How did you get that off of me without me feeling a thing?" I asked, completely amazed at how good she was.

Toya laughed. "It's not as hard as you think." She reached into another one of her pockets and asked, "What about this cheap MP3 player and this state ID with an ugly photo of you?"

"Damn," I said, checking all of my pockets to see what else I was missing.

"That's all I have. You're broke beyond belief," Toya said, placing all the electronic equipment back in the backpack. I gathered my belongings from her and tried to figure out when and how she'd taken them from me.

Toya rose to her feet and moved to the center of her bedroom. "Junior's father is into some of everything. He knows this old dude who used to be a magician."

"A magician? Like a person who does magic tricks?" I asked.

"Yes. But doing magic shows for kids didn't pay well, so the old dude used to make a killing by using card tricks as a way to distract people. He'd rip them off and hand their stuff to a second person who took them away. If a person would come back, he'd invite them to search his belongings and his pockets. But of course he wouldn't have anything, which left people totally confused as to where they'd lost their belongings. He never saved up any money and now that he's old and sickly, he's doing just about anything to make extra money and keep a roof over his head and pay for his prescription drugs. Anyway, dude took the time to teach me and my baby's daddy. I took all of your stuff from you while you stood at the front door. I kept you distracted with the other cell phone while I got close to you and searched your pockets. When I touched your hair with one hand, my other hand went into your pocket and pulled out your MP3 player and state ID. I tricked you and led you to believe I was truly interested in your hair. Misdirection is the key to doing it when you're close to someone. Since I actually touched your hair and that's where your focus was, you didn't notice my hand in your pocket."

"Dang," I said, totally tripping out by what she'd done.

"Stand up," Toya said. I did as she asked. Toya walked over to her closet and pulled out a fully dressed mannequin from the back of it. I started laughing.

"Where in the hell did you get that?" I asked as she pulled

it up next to me. "And it's an inflatable one—are you serious?"

"The magician sold it to me so I could practice with it. A lot of people keep stuff in their front shirt pocket. Using this mannequin I'll show you how to take stuff."

"Cool," I said, feeling a sense of excitement sweep over me.

"Remember, you have to be quick with your hands and you can't fumble or drop anything you're trying to take. If you do, quickly apologize and tell the person that it was hanging out and you were simply trying to catch it before it fell. Make them feel at ease, and as if you were only trying to help them. People will immediately say thank-you as you hand them back their belongings." Toya stuffed her cell phone in the front shirt pocket of the fully dressed mannequin.

"Now, try to take the phone," Toya instructed me.

"Okay," I said and pulled it out. It was very simple.

"No. You have to distract the mannequin through touch. Remember that, Viviana. You have to refocus the person's attention to something else or they're going to know what you're up to. Watch what I do." Toya demonstrated how to do it and then asked me to do the same thing.

"Good, but only slip one finger into the shirt pocket and press it against the fabric of the shirt pocket. This way the person doesn't feel you touching their chest." Toya continued to coach me. I did as she instructed and I was amazed at how easy it was. Toya and I spent more time practicing but we eventually had to stop because her son, Junior, had gotten restless. Since it was getting late, I decided to head upstairs to see how my mother was doing. My fear was that Martin would do something while I was away. The thought of her being beaten up made me rush out of Toya's apartment.

# five

Toya taught me a lot and I spent a significant amount of my time with her sharpening my pickpocketing skills. Eventually I was ready to try it out on someone other than Toya. My mother's boyfriend, Martin, seemed like the perfect test target. All I needed now was for the opportunity to present itself. Then, one late afternoon, it was as if Fate herself had heard my request and granted me my wish. Martin loved to drink beer and eat barbecue when he came home. The man barely needed a reason to fire up the grill and toss massive hunks of beef onto the open flames. I once heard him say he even enjoyed firing up the grill during the winter months when it was bitterly cold outside. I'd just walked in the door from Toya's apartment, where we'd been practicing and making plans to hit the Puerto Rican Day Festival in the Humboldt Park neighborhood the following day. Of course, I was very nervous, but when I saw Martin and my mother out on the back porch drinking and barbecuing I relaxed. It was good to see them in a pleasant mood. I saw it as my perfect opportunity. As I walked through the kitchen toward the back porch, I noticed Martin's massive back was turned toward me, and my mother was sitting on a worn-out chair situated far away enough from the grill that the smoke billowing up wouldn't irritate her eyes. I greeted them both and positioned myself so my mother couldn't see me reaching into his back pocket. I patted Martin on his back with an open hand and said, "What are you cooking?" Martin looked at me oddly. He probably figured I was up to something, because in general I wasn't very nice to him. We had come to a quiet understanding that I wouldn't mess with him as long as he didn't mess with me.

"Well, aren't you feeling friendly today," my mother said, noticing immediately that my behavior was peculiar.

"Well, Martin has the place smelling so good. I decided to come and see what the big guy was cooking," I said, trying to sound very sweet, innocent and nonthreatening.

"Bratwursts, Italian sausage and my favorite, steak burgers." Martin coughed as he flipped the meat over.

"Well, save some for me, I'm starving." I smiled as sweetly as I could, even though I hated the guy.

"Are you doing drugs?" Martin leaned toward me and looked deeply into my eyes.

"No," I said, slightly offended that he believed I'd stoop to such a low level. "I'm just trying to be nice," I said as I pretended to punch his big belly.

"That is so special, Viviana." My mother smiled gleefully. She fell for my line of crap hook, line and sinker. At times she could be so naive, especially when she felt as if she were in love or had found her soul mate yet again. If the truth were to be told, I also had a bone to pick with her, because I knew

Martin was the type of guy who'd eventually get physically abusive. However, for some reason that is beyond my comprehension, my mother viewed him as a gentle giant.

I pretended to not know the difference between a bratwurst and an Italian sausage and asked Martin to show me which was which. While he was distracted I reached for his wallet. I almost had it completely out of his pocket when I heard his stomach grumbling. Martin opened his mouth and let loose a very loud belch that reeked of bad breath and beer. The foul odor that passed through his lips was enough to make my stomach turn sour. I backed away from him, not wanting to go through the torture of inhaling another whiff of the foulness he'd released. As I moved away, I lost my grip on his wallet and it fell to the ground.

"It's better out than in," Martin said, just as his wallet flopped to the ground. He turned to see what the sound was.

"Why, you little—!"

Before Martin could finish his sentence I said, "I think your wallet fell," and reached for it.

"You were trying to rip me off!" Martin quickly lost his temper and I suddenly realized he was perhaps the last person I should have attempted to practice on. However, I didn't want him to think the worst of me, so I glanced at my mother, who was still trying to figure out what had set Martin off.

"No, I wasn't," I said, handing it over to him.

"I know that my wallet was deep inside my pocket, little girl!" Martin barked, so I moved away from him.

"Well, apparently it wasn't, because as soon as you belched it fell out of your pocket," I said, holding on to my lie.

My mother came over and took the wallet from me and placed it back inside Martin's rear pocket.

"Calm down, baby. Just be glad you didn't lose it on the street," my mother said, using her sweet caresses to calm her ogre down. I backed away from them.

"I've been around pickpockets before. I wasn't born yesterday." Martin shot bullets at me with his eyes.

"Whatever, man," I said, putting more distance between us. I went into my room and sat on the bed. It didn't take long for Martin to start verbally abusing my mother. I grabbed the knife I'd found and walked toward the back porch. I'd planned to stand watch in case he decided to put his hands on my mother. She eventually worked her charm and got him to calm down. Watching my mother bend over backward to soothe Martin's every tantrum was beyond irritating. She behaved as if her very existence depended on how happy he was. I eventually went into Martin's spare room and shut the door. I sat on the bed, exhaled, and then just glared at the floor as I thought about my father.

My dad was my world and there wasn't a day that went by that I didn't miss him. At times he'd tickle me to the point I'd almost pee on myself, but I didn't mind. Whenever he had the time he'd take me to a park on Chicago's lakefront and I'd play in the sand and splash around in the water. I was always bringing him something from beneath the sand or some object that had washed up on shore and he'd act as if it were the best gift in the world, which made me want to go find more stuff to give him. Dad loved playing softball and when I was nine he took me to the ballpark, where I'd watch him and all of his friends play. They were mostly guys from the neighborhood that he'd grown up with, but I considered them all to be my uncles because they never let anything happen to me. I always felt protected and safe around my father and his friends. My father had a reputation around the neighborhood, so no one dared to try to steal my bike if I left it on the sidewalk, or take candy from me. If someone tried, all I'd have to say was, "My father is Ricardo Vargas," and they'd immediately apologize. It was the coolest thing to have a father who everyone feared. The reason they feared him so much was beyond me, because the man that I knew was kind and gentle. He and my mother also loved going to parties and doing the bachata. Sometimes I'd watch them practice around the house because there was always a bachata dance contest going on and they'd won a lot of prize money together. Whenever they danced they looked like the perfect couple. They were so in love. Sometimes when they danced I'd get between them. Admittedly, I was a little jealous of my mother. I didn't want to share him with her.

Then one day my father came home bleeding. His forearm had been ripped open by a knife. When I saw all of the blood I just screamed because I thought he was dying.

"Viviana, go to your room!" He looked me directly in the eyes, but I was too afraid to leave him.

"No," I said with a trembling voice and eyes filled with tears.

"Go on, I'm okay, it's not as bad as it looks," he said, trying to comfort me. My mother was running around searching for the first aid kit. When she found it she gave it to my father, then escorted me to my room. She told me to go to bed and that everything was okay, but I didn't believe her.

I tried to run past her and go to my father, but she stopped me. She pushed me back inside the room and locked the door from the outside. I kicked the door and screamed at the top of my lungs. I screamed and yelled until my voice was gone. Finally, I fell asleep on the floor.

When I awoke the next morning, I was in my bed and my bedroom door was cracked open. I walked out and found my father in the kitchen, drinking orange juice directly from the cartoon. His arm was bandaged up and he said, "See, I'm fine." I wanted to ask him what happened but I didn't. I just walked over to him and hugged him as tightly as I could.

"I'm going to teach you how to protect yourself. You're ten years old now and you're getting to be a big girl."

"Protect myself from what? All I have to do is mention your name and people leave me alone," I said.

"I know, but sometimes that may not be enough, and I may not always be around to scare off the bad guys. Let me see you make a fist." I did what he said.

"You have strong hands like me. I'll show you how to fight and protect yourself like a boy. That way you'll fight differently than a girl," he said.

"But why?" I asked once again.

"Because you just never know, a lot of things can happen out there on the streets and I want my little girl to know how to handle herself," he explained.

Thinking about my father caused my emotions to get carried away and the last thing I wanted to do was break down crying. I pushed my pain deep down and pressed my palms to my eyes. As I did this I could hear my father's ghostly voice telling me to toughen up.

★ ★ ★

The following day I left the house before my mother and Martin awoke. I knew that my mother didn't really care where I was going, and I damn sure knew that Martin didn't. I knocked on Toya's door and waited for her to answer it. When Toya opened the door she had a black scarf tied around her hair, some baggy gym shorts and a tank top with the words *What Are You Looking At?* typed across her bosom.

"Damn, yo' ass is up early. Are you that frantic to get to do this?" Toya threaded her eyebrows and frowned.

"I had a bad night and needed to get out of that house," I explained as I followed her to her room.

"It's cool, I understand." Toya gazed at what I was wearing.

"At least you don't have on those damn flip-flops today," she said before entering the bathroom. I continued on to her bedroom and sat on a chair positioned against her window. Her son was in the bed asleep on his back, so I wanted to make sure I remained quiet. When Toya returned she was unwrapping her head scarf.

"Who is going to watch your baby for you today?" I asked.

"His daddy is coming over to get him," Toya said as she yawned.

"What time is he coming?" I asked. Toya glanced at an alarm clock that read 10:45 a.m.

"He should be here by noon," she said, moving around the room and getting dressed. Once she was dressed she pulled out two duffel bags and tossed one to me.

"I have an extra one. You can use it," she said. "That way there's no confusion about who earned what today."

"So, not only do I have to lift stuff, I have to carry my things," I said, taking the bag.

"You're on your own, girl. Everyone has to start somewhere. We'll each work opposite sides of the street. When you reach the end of the street, turn around and make another pass. After that, head home and we'll meet back here," Toya said.

"I'm nervous as hell," I confessed.

"I was nervous my very first time, too, but you'll get over it, I promise." Toya tried to ease my fears.

"Here." She tossed me her stun gun. "You can have it. My boyfriend is bringing me a new one when he comes to pick up his son."

"Thank you," I said, turning it on to make sure that it was fully charged. I was going to leave it with Toya until we returned, but decided to toss it into the bag she'd given me.

By the time Toya and I arrived, the festival was in full swing. The streets were lined with white tents where vendors sold their merchandise and there was a massive crowd of people. Music seemed to be coming from every direction and no matter where I turned there was something going on. Either someone was paying for a souvenir, buying food or watching the street performers.

"This is perfect and should be easy pickings because there are plenty of distractions." Toya purposely spoke into my ear.

"I see that," I said, fascinated by the spectacle of it all.

"This is where we part ways. I'll see you back at my place later tonight. Hopefully, we'll both earn enough cash and prizes to make our pockets fat." Toya grinned like a very satisfied cat. "Good luck," she said and walked away.

I adjusted my duffel bag, which was slung over one shoulder, and began walking through the crowd. The event was without question one that brought together many people from different cultures. Black, white, Latino and Asian. As I made my way through the throngs of people, I spotted a man wearing a red, white and blue summer short set with Puerto Rico spelled out across the back of his shoulders. He was riding a bicycle with a trailer hitch, towing two barrels of Popsicles he was selling. I thought he'd make a good target but I'd have to wait until he got off the bike. After following him for a while, I decided to move on and find some other person, because it would be too much trouble to pick his pockets. As I continued on I saw people carrying backpacks that they'd forgotten to zip up, women with purses that were wide open, and men with money sitting in the breast pockets of their shirts. All I had to do was time my move perfectly. I came upon a gathering of people who were watching sidewalk performers. As I got closer, I saw that the performers were from a local dance studio. There were four women, all dressed in yellow T-shirts and blue jeans, banging on some bongos and singing in perfect rhythm. There was another woman from the organization who was dancing to the rhythmic sounds. Everyone was focused on the performers, including myself. It wasn't until someone brushed past me to get a closer look that I remembered I wasn't there to watch the show. I was there to get paid. I stepped back from the crowd and noticed a cluster of girls. One of them was wearing a backpack that hung low and rested on her butt.

She was the perfect target. The bag wasn't zipped fully and I saw that her wallet was exposed.

"This is going to be so easy," I mumbled to myself. I moved closer to the girl and her friends and acted as if I was trying to view the performance. I nudged the girl, who turned and looked at me. She looked to be about my age. She had black hair with very pale skin. Judging by the way she glared at me, I knew if I didn't speak up quickly, she'd take my nudging her as a sign of disrespect and start a brawl.

"Excuse me. I'm sorry, I was just trying to get a better look." I smiled as I delicately unzipped her backpack a little more. I looked behind me to map out my escape route when I noticed the man on the bicycle selling Popsicles was about to roll past. The girl turned her attention back to the performer and I eased my fingers inside her backpack and easily slid her wallet out. Before I could tuck the wallet away, the girl turned and said, "Hey, I want a Popsicle." The girl removed her backpack. I tried to step away but the bicycle and the crowd of people were blocking me.

"Hey, why do you have my damn wallet in your hand!" The girl quickly realized what I'd done. I pushed another woman out of the way and bolted like a flash of lightning. The girl and her friend chased after me. I pushed my way around people and even knocked down a little girl. I glanced over my shoulder and there were at least two girls coming after me. I thought about dropping the wallet, but at that moment I saw an opening in the crowd. I ran toward it as fast as I could, then made a quick left and ran down a side street away from the festival. Once again I glanced over my shoulder and the girls were still coming after me. I cut between two apartment buildings and leaned against one of the structures to catch my breath. I heard one of the girls say, "There she is!" I started running again, racing through a backyard and out into an alley. Looking right and then left, not knowing which way to run. I finally turned to my right and ran as fast as my legs would take me. The alley let out onto a main street. I saw a bus coming and raced toward the corner to catch it. The bus pulled over at the stoplight. The driver opened the door and I stepped on. I took my duffel bag off my shoulder before taking a seat, totally out of breath. Unzipping my bag, I pulled out my bus card and paid my fare. I then started making my way toward the rear of the bus and took a seat, but noticed the bus was empty with the exception of a few elderly people sitting toward the front. I also noticed that the bus wasn't moving. The driver had been caught by a red light. I decided to open the wallet I'd taken from the girl to take a look at what was in it. I found the girl's identification. Her name was Liz Lloyd. I checked another compartment and removed the money. I had two one-hundred-dollar bills and a few singles. I smiled, happy with the score. At that moment I heard a loud thudding sound. When I looked out the window I saw that the girls had found me.

"Oh, crap!" I said, grabbing my duffel bag. I was hoping the bus driver would pull off, but he didn't. Instead he opened the doors and the girls rushed toward me. I tried to beat them to the rear door so that I could dash off but it was too late and they were on me. Fists seemed to be coming at me from all directions. I dropped my duffel and defended myself as best I could. One girl pulled my hair while the other one took turns hitting me with hammer fists. I swung back but my punches were ineffective. I thought for a moment that some other passenger or at least the bus driver would come to my aid, but no one did. I fell to the floor.

"You're lucky I got my wallet back!" Liz Lloyd barked before she and her friend nailed me with a barrage of kicks that landed in my gut and on my back. I noticed my stun gun had fallen out of my bag and was on the floor underneath a seat in front of me. I reached for it and turned it on. As best as I could, I held on to a leg of one of the girls and zapped her. She screamed as her body shook violently. It didn't take much for her to fall. Liz kicked me once more before checking on her friend. I was exhausted and could barely stand up. Liz and her friend tried to get off the bus but the driver had locked all the doors and called the police. Liz pulled the emergency handle on the window and crawled out. As she wormed her way out the window, I zapped her hands with the stun gun. She screamed as she tumbled to the ground. Her friend begged the bus driver to open the door and let her off, which he did.

"I've called the police. Are you okay?" the bus driver asked.

I didn't answer him. I grabbed my bag and headed for the rear door. I tried to push it open but it wouldn't budge.

"Let me off!" I yelled up front toward the driver. He released the door lock and I walked off. I was starting to wonder if I had what it took to make it as a pickpocket.

# SIX

*MAYA*

It was early afternoon and I was sitting at the edge of the swimming pool with my legs submerged in water up to my knees. My ankle was near one of the water vents and the pulsation of the water jetting out of the spout felt really good against my leg. I'd decided to come and hang out with Keysha, who was busy vacuuming the bottom of the swimming pool and fussing about all the things the lifeguard on duty the night before hadn't done. I was only partially listening to her because my mind, of course, was on my beloved Misalo. I wanted to rake my fingers through his hair, kiss him on the lips and hold him close. At times I just felt as if my world was completely empty without him. Misalo in many ways defined who I was.

"Maya." Keysha called my name and snapped me out of my daydream. I looked in her direction and she pointed to the vacuum hose, which had gotten tangled up around a lawn chair.

"Oh, I'll get it," I said as I lifted myself onto my feet.

"What were you just thinking about?" Keysha asked as I fixed the issue with the hose.

"Misalo." I sighed depressingly.

"Do you really miss him that much?" she asked as I walked toward her.

"Yes. We're soul mates. He's so understanding and considerate and..."

"Okay. I understand." Keysha cut me off and I didn't know how to take her rudeness.

"What's that supposed to mean?" I was all posed to become really upset with her. I mean, I sat around and listened to her and all of the chaos she went through with three different guys and never once complained.

"Nothing," Keysha quickly answered, but I could tell that she wasn't being totally truthful with me.

"No. You wanted to say something. I could tell. Say what's on your mind. I need to hear it." I pressed the issue.

"Maya, don't you feel like you're a little obsessed with Misalo? You talk about him endlessly." I couldn't believe Keysha had just said that to me, especially after how I'd been by her side.

"You're jealous, aren't you?"

"No. Don't be silly. I'm not jealous. Why would I be?"

"Because you don't have a boyfriend and none of your relationships have ever worked out since I've known you."

"That was a low blow, Maya." Keysha had a very sad look in her eyes.

"Well, what you said to me just now was a low blow."

Keysha sighed, then stopped and looked me directly in the eyes. "Okay, perhaps I'm just a little envious, but it's not like

I'm trying to break you guys up or anything. I just want to talk about other things and do more girl stuff," Keysha explained.

"Heck, I wanted to do the same things when I met you and all you did was talk about your relationships, but I didn't say anything because I knew it would hurt your feelings," I explained.

"Did I really have a one-track mind?" Keysha asked.

"Does Lil Wayne have tattoos?" I said as I rolled my neck. Keysha chuckled.

"Okay, I'm sorry for what I said. I didn't mean to upset you." Keysha put the vacuum pole down and gave me a hug.

I was reluctant about returning the gesture but it didn't take me long to let go of my attitude.

"Hey, we've got company." Keysha stepped away from me and nodded in the direction of the doorway. I turned to see who was there and, to my dismay, Lori, the neighborhood gossip girl, had just walked in with some guy I'd never seen before.

"Whose life is she about to ruin now?" I asked.

"I don't know the guy's name. I've only seen him here once before. He didn't swim much the last time he came in."

"Who was he here with the last time you saw him?" I asked, noticing how tall and muscular he was. He was a Mexican guy who looked to be around the same age as Keysha and I. He had short black hair, a pencil-thin mustache and walked with a very pronounced and cocky swagger.

"No one—he just showed up and sat down. He put his iPod earphones in, placed his sunglasses over his eyes and just chilled out," Keysha explained.

"He's kind of cute," I said.

"I thought you were madly in love already." I could tell by the tone of Keysha's voice she was surprised that I was checking the guy out.

"There is nothing wrong with looking." I laughed quietly. "But I feel sorry for him if he's hanging around Lori," I added.

"I don't think he's with Lori. They just may have walked in at the same time. Look, they're not even sitting with each other," Keysha pointed out.

"Well, it probably won't be long before she takes her skinny behind and starts parading it around in front of his face," I said, as if I'd already seen Lori doing it.

"Lori just makes me sick!" Keysha said as she continued to do her job.

"You should go talk to the guy and act like you're really interested in him, just to tick her off," I suggested, feeling a little catty.

"That would be funny, wouldn't it?" Keysha asked.

"Yes. Go on and ask him his name before that slut does," I said, encouraging her. Keysha made her way around to the other side of the pool where the guy was. I walked back to my lawn chair where my beach towel, cell phone and purse were. Just as I was about to place my legs back in the water and watch Keysha irritate the hell out of Lori, I heard my cell phone ringing. I quickly moved to answer it.

"Hey, baby," I answered, once I realized it was Misalo.

"What's going on?" Misalo asked.

"Nothing, just hanging out with my girl, Keysha. What are you up to?" I asked playfully as I smiled from ear to ear.

"Wondering where you are because I want to come see you," he said.

"You can't come see me. You're in California and you're not coming home for another two days."

"Actually, we came home early. My father and grandfather got into an argument. It's a long story but I just wanted to let you know that I'm home now."

"OMG! This is so perfect," I said, feeling tingly all over.

"Do you want me to come to the swimming pool?" he asked.

"No. Meet me at my house in ten minutes," I said cheerfully.

"I thought your dad hated me and didn't want me around you." Misalo jogged my memory.

"Both he and my mom are at work. They won't be home for hours. It's perfectly fine. Just meet me there. We have a lot of unfinished business to catch up on," I said as I began gathering my belongings.

"Okay. I'll see you in a few minutes," Misalo said just before I hung up the phone. I glanced back at Keysha, who was smiling while talking to the new guy.

"Keysha!" I yelled. She turned to look at me.

"Misalo is back. I'm going to go see him," I said.

"Don't go and get yourself knocked up!" Lori yelled out before Keysha could say goodbye. I gave Lori the most evil glare that I could before flipping her my middle finger. Lori waved me off.

"Call me later," I heard Keysha say as I headed toward the exit.

★ ★ ★

By the time I arrived back at home, Misalo was sitting in the driveway on his bicycle waiting for me. I felt as if my legs couldn't get him to me fast enough and before I knew it I rushed toward him. I wrapped my arms around him and kissed him, almost toppling him over.

"Hey, you." I pulled back and looked into his eyes.

"It's good to see you, too," he said as he dismounted his bike.

"Come on, I'll open up the garage. You can leave your bike in there," I said. Once his bike was put away, we entered the house holding hands. As I led him through the kitchen I ran into Anna and my little brother, Paul, who were in the kitchen making a mess, trying to cook themselves something to eat.

"Ooo, I'm telling," Anna blurted.

"You're going to tell what?" I asked in a threatening tone of voice.

"You know we're not supposed to have people in the house when Mom and Dad are not here." Anna forced me to recall our parents silly little rule.

"Rules were made to be broken, Anna." I continued to pull Misalo along behind me.

"I'm going to call Dad right now," Anna said, forcing me to deal with her.

I stopped, looked at Misalo and said, "You remember where my room is, don't you?"

"Yes," he answered with a huge smile.

"Go wait for me there," I said as I smacked his butt.

Misalo glanced at Anna and said, "Don't be such a brat, okay?"

Once Misalo was gone, I turned to Anna and lowered my eyelids to slits. I knuckled up my fist and held it close to Anna's chin.

"If you even think about calling Dad, I will beat you while you're sleeping," I threatened.

"Tell her you're not afraid of her, Anna," said Paul, my eleven-year-old brother, who only encouraged Anna because he wanted to see us fight.

"I'm not afraid of you, Maya," Anna said defiantly.

"Even if you did call Dad, he wouldn't believe you. I'd just tell him you're lying and that you have no proof."

"Paul will say it's true." Anna looked in the direction of our brother.

"Paul," I growled his name. "You're not going to say a word, are you?" I gave him my most evil glare, something that I'd been doing ever since he was little. It was my special way of manipulating him.

"No," he immediately answered.

"See, Anna, you have nothing on me," I said confidently as I stepped away.

"You make me sick, Maya," she snarled.

"The feeling is mutual," I said, laughing as I ran up the stairs to spend time with my honey. When I walked into my room, Misalo was standing near a window.

"Are you looking for someone?" I asked, trying to sound seductive. Misalo tried to laugh suavely as he moved toward me. We met in the center of the room and I forced him down on my bed.

"I'm not playing games," I said as I straddled his legs, resting my behind on his thighs and pushing his shoulders downward toward my mattress. Misalo now lay flat on his back.

"You really have missed me." He had a huge grin on his face.

"I'm about to show you just how much I've missed you." I ran my fingers through his hair. Misalo lifted himself up and rested on his elbows. I leaned in to kiss him. Our lips met, and our tongues danced in circles. I was so hopelessly lost in the moment that I didn't hear Anna creep into my room.

"I've got you now!" Anna shouted. I leaped off Misalo so quickly I nearly got whiplash.

"I took a picture of you trying to suck his face off," Anna said, laughing like a wicked witch.

"Anna, you totally need to grow the hell up. Get out of my room!" I screamed.

"No! Unless I get paid, I'm telling Mom and Dad, and delivering them proof that you had Misalo in your room." Anna closed her flip phone, folded her arms across her bosom, and shifted her weight from one foot to the other.

"I don't believe you took a picture," I snarled.

"Check your email. I just sent it to you so you'll know that I'm for real," Anna said smugly. I grabbed my cell phone, which was connected to my email account. Sure enough, I had a message from Anna.

"Why are you so mean to your sister?" Misalo asked Anna.

"Because she's wrong and she knows it," Anna answered him.

"Don't you have a secret boyfriend of some kind?" Misalo asked, clearly just as annoyed with Anna as I was.

"I'm only fourteen. I can't date boys yet." Anna's voice was filled with contempt.

After looking at the photo, which I knew would cause my father to go into a rage if he saw it, I turned to Anna and said, "What do you want?"

"Money," she answered.

"How much money?" I asked. Anna paused for a moment, then laughed.

"Four hundred dollars," she blurted.

"Anna, I don't have that kind of money," I said through gritted teeth. I wanted to lunge at her, wrestle her cell phone away and then smash it.

"I figured you wouldn't have it. That's why I copied Mom and Dad on the email anyway."

"No you didn't," I said, thinking that there was no way Anna could be that spiteful.

"Check for yourself. Once Daddy sees you all over Misalo, he'll realize that you're not the perfect princess that he thinks you are. I'd certainly hate to be in your shoes right now." Anna laughed, then offered up a sinister smile. I once again checked my phone and looked at who she'd copied and, sure enough, Anna had copied our parents.

"You little witch!" I tossed my cell phone on the bed and lunged toward Anna. I was about to issue her a major beat down. Anna decided to be brave and stand her ground. She waited for me to get close to her before she began churning her arms like a windmill. She was hoping that I'd walk into one of her punches. I easily got around her defense and pulled at her hair.

"Why, you little freaking annoying and pesky girl!" I slung her thin body from right to left.

"Let me go!" she shouted, but I didn't. I was way too angry with her. I began pounding her body with hammer fists. Anna pulled herself away from me and threw a kick that nailed me on the thigh. She then swung wildly and landed another shot on my cheek.

"I hate you!" she howled as she continued to swing and miss. Misalo made a move to stop us but I waved him off. I grabbed Anna's hair and yanked really hard, causing her head and neck to twist into an awkward position.

"Maya!" Misalo yelled my name, which forced both Anna and I to stop. Misalo approached me, holding up my buzzing cell phone.

"Who is it?" I asked, utterly aggravated.

"It says Dad on the caller ID screen." Misalo glanced at me nervously.

Frustrated, I growled as I took the phone from Misalo and attempted to calm my nerves.

"Hey, Daddy." I tried to sound happy, as if nothing was going on. I thought I'd at least get a chance to explain the photo or stall him long enough to come up with a good lie. Rather than hear my side of the story, my father exploded with unbridled anger.

"What the hell is going on with you, Maya? Why do you have that boy in the house when you know your mother and I have forbid it!"

"Dad, I have a life, too! And Anna—" My dad cut me off before I could finish my sentence.

"I'll deal with Anna later. I'm not happy that you've disrespected my home and allowed that boy to disrespect it, as well!" I'd never heard my father sound this angry before.

"What about the trust that Anna has broken with me? I do have a right to privacy, don't I?"

"Are you doing drugs? Because you sound like you've lost your damn mind! You're only sixteen—your privacy is my business!" I could tell by the way he kept raising his voice that I was digging my own grave.

"Daddy, I'm in love. Why can't you see that?" I held back the tears swirling around in my heart like a cyclone.

"Maya, you're not in love. Judging by this photo, you're deeply in lust and you can easily slip up and become a teen mother. Now, my job as your father is to prevent you from making that mistake. I hope he was worth the ass-whooping you've got coming for pulling this stunt."

"Why can't you understand my feelings for Misalo?"

"Maya, you don't know jack squat about love. That's the problem with your generation. You think you know every damn thing but can't tell the difference between sunrise and sunset!" my father fired back.

"How can you say that? How can you say that my feelings aren't real?" His comment hurt me in a way that I hadn't anticipated.

"Is that boy still there?" My dad avoided answering my question by asking one of his own.

"No, Misalo is gone now," I lied.

"No, he's not. You never could lie to me, Maya." He paused for a moment. "I'm going to call Anna now, and if she tells me that guy is still there, you're going to have hell to pay when I get there."

"Why do you believe everything she says?" I uncharacteristically challenged his authority and his apparent preference of Anna over me.

"You should learn how to be more like your little sister. Anna is a good girl who isn't sneaking boys into the house behind my back, and she isn't sneaking off to wild parties and returning home with broken bones."

"So, do you think Anna is better than me? She isn't that wonderful, Dad. She does her share of dirt, too, but you just don't know about it," I said, wanting to get Anna in just as much trouble as I was in.

"Maya, this conversation is over until your mother and I get home. In fact, I'm leaving the office right now. I'll see you shortly," my dad said, and then he hung up on me.

I held my cell phone in my hand for a moment before I exhaled and then screamed. It didn't take long for my tears to come.

"Baby, what's wrong? What did he say?" Misalo embraced me and stroked my back. I buried my face in his chest and sobbed.

"Nothing is working out the way I envisioned it. I had the perfect afternoon planned and now everything is ruined."

"It's going to be okay." Misalo tried to reassure me but his words were filled with empty promises.

"Let's just run away," I suggested. "We'll show everyone just how strong true love is. We'll show them that there is only one person that each of us is meant to be with. For me, I know that person is you." I stepped away and looked into Misalo's eyes. "Don't you feel the same way?"

"You know that I do," he agreed.

"Then tell me. I need to know that no matter what, some-way, somehow, we'll be together and no one or nothing can tear us apart." I waited for his response as if my heart would stop beating if he didn't feel the same way.

"Maya, from the moment I first met you, I knew that you were special. I want the same things that you want and I'll do anything to prove it." Misalo kissed me.

"My father said you didn't love me because you took me to an unsafe and inhumane dogfight," I whispered as I smeared away more tears.

Misalo embraced me once again. "That's ridiculous. He just doesn't want to realize that you're a woman now. Sooner or later he is going to have to come around and respect our relationship." Misalo held me tightly and it felt warm and beautiful like the blending of the sea and sky.

"Excuse me, Maya." It was my little brother, Paul. "You may want to get him out of here really fast. I just got off the phone with Mom and she's just up the street stuck waiting for the freight train to pass."

"Oh, my God! Hurry up, Misalo! You've got to get out of here. If she sees you I'll never hear the end of it." Misalo wasted no time rushing out of my room. He retrieved his bike from the garage, mounted it and took off as fast as he could before my mother arrived.

# seven

*VIVIANA*

when I returned to the apartment I was so thankful my mother and her boyfriend, Martin, were not there, because I really didn't feel like answering a bunch of questions about why my face looked the way it did. My bottom lip was split down the middle, and my face was bruised in several places. Most of the damage could be hidden with makeup, so in a way I was thankful for that. I went into the bathroom, took a shower and went about the business of hiding my war wounds. When I was finished I stared at myself in the mirror. All of my blemishes were well concealed, but I didn't like my reflection. I felt as if I were a train wreck that no one really cared about. I got angry and let out a scream.

"You're such a lost cause, Viviana!" I spat at my own reflection.

Wringing my hands I said, "Maybe you should hurt yourself. Perhaps then someone would care." The thought of allowing my mind to slip into madness was a tempting one.

When I finished mentally beating myself up, a feeling of claustrophobia came over me. I suddenly felt as if the walls were caving in on me. The musty odor of the apartment made my stomach turn sour and my skin felt as if there were millions of tiny ants crawling all over it. I began scratching my arms, my hair and my stomach with my fingernails. I shouted at the top of my voice again as I walked out of the bathroom with only a towel wrapped around my body, feeling as if I were about to lose my mind. I decided to stand still in an attempt to calm myself.

"Get a grip, Viviana," I said, trying to reassure myself that I was safe and that I was okay. I took a few deep breaths and said, "I have to get out of here." I rushed back into my bedroom and put on some clothes. Racing out of the apartment, I took the back stairwell, and left through the rear exit. Without giving much thought to what I was going to do or where I was headed, I started walking east toward the lakefront. Mindlessly, I walked, not really thinking about much of anything except that I had to keep moving. I made it to the shoreline of Lake Michigan and sat on a sandy beach near the Museum of Science and Industry. Kicking my shoes off, I placed my feet on the hot sand. I coiled my knees to my chest and wrapped my arms around them. Listening to the roar of the water as it crashed against the shoreline was calming. I glanced around at all of the people there. It was mostly parents playing with their kids and the family dog. I thought about my father again and about how much I missed him and how I wished I could turn back the hands of time and talk to him. How I longed to hear his voice laughing. I wanted to dance with him in the middle of the floor and hug him so I could feel safe and protected.

I pulled out my cell phone and scrolled through my photos until I found one of the two of us together. It had been taken several years before. Around the time our lives begun to spiral out of control. He didn't smile as much as he used to. In fact, he hated for anyone to take a photo of him, but he took one for me because it was my birthday. I scrolled to the next picture I had of us. I was about eight years old. My mom came into my bedroom and took a picture of my dad and me playing with my Lilo and Stitch dolls. We were both sitting on the floor making the dolls walk and run and jump and play. He always made the dolls talk for me, and he was talented in giving them different voices. I scrolled through and found one last family photo taken at Walmart. I was two years old, and my parents and I were wearing matching Chicago Bulls championship T-shirts from 1996. I remember my dad being a huge Michael Jordan fan. I forced back tears by shutting my eyes and took a deep breath. After a moment I opened my eyes and closed my phone and forced myself to stop thinking about my dad. He was gone and no amount of wishing was going to ever bring him back.

The following day I caught up with Toya, who wanted to know how much money and merchandise I'd scored. We went into her bedroom so that I could give her the details of how I'd gotten jacked up. When I told her what had gone down, her mouth opened as wide as the ocean.

"Are you serious? Two chicks chased you onto a city bus and jumped you?" Toya was intrigued by the brawl I had.

"Yeah, and if it hadn't been for the stun gun you gave me, I'd probably be in an emergency room all messed up."

"Damn. That's jacked up," Toya said sympathetically.

"Sometimes stuff like that happens, though. You just have to learn from your mistake and move on, that's all."

"Yeah, that's easier said than done," I said. Toya moved closer to inspect my bruises.

"What did your mother say about your face?" she asked me.

"Nothing. She doesn't know. Even if she did notice, I don't think she'd care much. She's too busy trying to keep her new man happy. She's not very concerned about me, and I can pretty much do anything I want to as long as I don't bring another mouth in the house to feed." I paused in thought for a moment. "I wish there was a way for me to have a normal life."

Toya chuckled. "People like us will never have a normal life. We're from the 'hood. The moment we were born, our lives jumped on an express elevator to hell. We're never going to get out of here, so we've got to make the best of it and do what we've gotta do in order to survive. Don't you agree?" Toya asked.

"Of course I do. My father told me the same thing," I said.

"You want to know what I was thinking?" The tone of Toya's voice was suddenly upbeat.

"No?" I answered.

"We could probably make a killing if we were to go downtown and target businesspeople. We could get all types of credit cards and cash. Plus, I'm sure they're not going to chase us onto a city bus."

"That does sound like a sweet plan," I said, thinking about the possibilities.

"So, are you down with doing that?" she asked.

"Yeah, count me in. I don't have anything else to do anyway," I said, allowing the weight of my misery to dictate my decision.

"Cool, we'll hook up tomorrow and take the bus downtown."

"Where will we go? I mean, we can't just walk into an office building."

Toya laughed. "Oh, yes we can."

"What? Are you crazy? I'm not going to walk into an office building and pick someone's pocket." I thought for sure Toya had lost her mind.

"No. I'm not saying that we're going to do it. I just know of people who are brave enough to do that kind of job. They dress up like regular businesspeople and walk from floor to floor acting like they're trying to raise money for a cause. You'd be surprised at how easily people will give up money when you say it's to help build a community center or some other nonsense about making a neighborhood better. I know this one girl who made two thousand dollars in a matter of a few hours."

"Are you serious?" I couldn't believe someone had made that type of money off of a scam.

"Yeah. She wants to bring me in on it, but told me that I needed to learn how to speak better."

"Speak better?" I asked, confused.

"You know. Sound all proper and stuff. I told her, 'I can't be talking like I got a college degree or something. I'm a high school dropout and proud of it.' She told me that she dropped out of school in eighth grade, but she can sound like she has a degree from Harvard when she wants to. Anyway, I told her that I didn't like talking to strange people that much and preferred to just take what I needed from them. It's simpler. I'll introduce you to her one day. Her name is Elva, but everyone calls her Penny."

"I would like to meet her. She sounds like she's really cool," I said.

"She is. Penny has an entire crew that does stuff like that," Toya explained.

"How do you know all of these people?" I asked.

"I know all types of people. It's like we have our own secret social network." Toya beamed with pride. "Anyway, I hate to put you out, but I promised my grandmother I'd go with her to church. She's trying to save my soul." Toya laughed.

"I don't believe you go church," I said.

"Yes, I do. You'd be surprised by how much money I get when I go there," Toya joked.

"Isn't that like sacred ground?" I felt like that was a line I'd probably never cross.

"Oh, don't worry. I do thank Jesus for placing people with money in my path." Toya laughed out loud.

"Okay. On that note, I'm going to head back upstairs." I rose to my feet and headed toward the door.

"I'll send you a text tomorrow morning to let you know when I'm ready to head downtown. I'm thinking we could hit some of those really busy food courts during the lunch hour. Women are always leaving their purse draped on the back of a chair for one reason or another. That's a perfect

time to move in and slip it off the chair without them noticing."

"Sounds like a plan to me." I nodded in agreement before
heading toward the front door.

# eight

*MAYA*

I thought I was so clever because I was able to get Misalo out of the house without my mother seeing him. I was confident I'd be able to somehow make my father believe that the photo he had seen of me and Misalo was really nothing to be upset over. Even if I had to break down and cry to soften him up, I knew I was witty enough to pull it off. When all of the drama settled down, I was going to make Anna pay big-time. My plan was to not get mad or even with her, I was going to get ahead of her. I just had to be patient and nail her when she least expected it. If she wanted to make our father believe I was the neighborhood slut, then I was determined to make him believe she was the community crackhead. However, with all of the scheming and plotting that I was mapping out in my mind, what I did not factor into my equation was my mother.

When she arrived home she was on the phone with my father discussing what my punishment should be. The way she looked at me when she walked into the house made me realize she was ticked off enough to drown a woman on dry land. I wasn't going to get around her so easily.

"Oh, don't worry. I'm going to deal with both of them right now," I heard my mother say as she tossed her keys and purse on the countertop. I exhaled loudly because I knew I was in for a long lecture. The moment my mother heard my groaning, she popped her fingers and then angrily pointed at one of the kitchen chairs, motioning me to park my rear end at the table.

I sat and continued to eavesdrop on my mother's phone conversation with my father. "I know. It was extremely disrespectful, and while Anna was busy digging a hole for Maya to fall into she doesn't realize that she's also dug one for herself. Okay. I'll see you when you get here," my mother said. As soon as she was off the phone I began talking.

"It really isn't as bad as it looks," I said, trying to extinguish the blaze in my mother's eyes.

"Maya, shut up!" she hissed at me. I folded my arms and did as I was told.

"Anna!" my mother yelled out, but got no response. She moved toward the living room and stood in the archway between the two rooms. "Anna!"

"Huh?" I heard my sister answer back.

"Huh, my foot! Get down here." My mother sounded like an angry drill sergeant. She walked back into the kitchen and glared at me. If she had a samurai's sword I knew she'd take at least one swing at my neck. Anna finally arrived and sat on a chair at the opposite side of the table.

"What's going on with you two?" my mother asked.

I shrugged my shoulders. "Ask her, she started it."

"I didn't start anything!" Anna barked. "You're the one who's always bossing me around like you think you own me. And you're always in my room borrowing my clothes and jewelry."

"Mom, she is lying through her teeth. We don't even have the same style and I definitely wouldn't wear any of her funky clothes that she leaves piled up in the corner of her room. Have you looked in her room lately? I'll bet a million bucks that there is some type of fungus growing in there."

"See, that proves that she's been in my room and invading my privacy!" Anna snapped back.

"Are you serious! You're the one who invaded my privacy, you little—"

"Maya!" my mother once again barked. Before I had a chance to say what I really wanted to I huffed and cut my eyes at Anna.

"The feeling is mutual," Anna said, trying to get in the last word.

"Whatever!" I said, wishing I could flip up my middle finger at her.

"Enough!" My mother, as usual got in the last word. "You girls are bickering over petty things. And I'm disappointed with both of you. Anna, the email photograph that you sent to your father was disrespectful."

"How else was I going to prove that she was breaking the rules? You guys never believe me. You always take Maya's side because she's the oldest," Anna complained.

"Mom, that's not true. Don't listen to her," I said.

"Maya, if I hear another word from you, you will be writing a check that your behind can't cash. Shut up!" I listened to my mother and remained silent, but in my mind I was confused. One minute she's asking me what was going on between Anna and me, and when I try to explain, she's threatening me with violence.

"I believe I have a clear picture of what's going on here. You two are fighting like the Hatfields and McCoys," she said, trying to put our rivalry in simple terms.

"Who are the Hatfields and McCoys?" Anna stupidly asked.

"Not too bright, are you?" I murmured. The moment the words escaped my lips I felt my mother slap the back of my head. I didn't even see the hit coming. I swallowed my tears of humiliation; I wasn't about to let Anna see me cry. The hit itself didn't really sting. It was the fact that my mother was angry enough to do it that hurt more.

"You two are fighting just like my sister, Salena, and I did when we were young. We were always competing with each other for attention. The only thing the rivalry did was build a valley between us, and I will not allow that to happen with you two. Anna, no loving father wants to see his daughter making out with a boy, or man, for that matter. By sending that photo you've hurt him in a way that is not easily put into words."

"I was only trying to show everyone how sneaky she is." Anna defended her actions.

"Little girl, did you hear what I just said?" My mother glared at Anna with disbelief in her eyes. "Don't *ever* send anything like that to your father again."

"He should be mad at Maya, not me." Anna didn't have the good sense to shut up.

"Anna, a hard head makes for a soft behind." My mother kept trying to provide Anna with a little wisdom. But as always, Anna just didn't get it.

"Huh?" Anna asked.

"Your stubbornness will be your downfall." My mother gave Anna a look of damnation.

"This is so not fair," Anna whined. A truly twisted part of me was very happy that she was in just as much hot water as I was.

"Maya." My mother turned her attention to me. "You've really lost your mind. What were you thinking? Why would you even think that it was okay to have a boy over when we're not home?"

I shrugged as if I were dumb. I certainly wasn't about to tell her the truth, which was that I was feeling neglected and wanted to make out with my boyfriend.

"Are you trying to get pregnant?" she asked. I didn't answer her because she'd told me twice to shut up.

"You hear me talking to you! Answer me!" my mother snapped.

"No," I quickly said before she decided to do something more drastic.

"Then what were you thinking?"

I honestly didn't know what to tell her. But then, in the back of my mind I heard a little voice whisper to me, *Tell her you're in love.*

"I love him, Mom, and love makes you do crazy things." I felt as if I'd given her a rock-solid answer that could not be challenged.

"Love! Honey, you're only sixteen and haven't lived long

enough to understand love. Love is what's keeping me from putting a bullet between your eyes right now.

"You're in lust," she concluded with a tone full of disappointment. My mother exhaled and combed her fingers through her hair. She then placed her hands on her hips.

"Anna, leave. Go to your room. I'll be up there soon." Anna looked at me and rolled her eyes before leaving. My mother sat next to me and leaned back, resting her arm on the back of the chair.

"Look at you. You think you have the world by the tail. You believe that you've got everything all figured out. I've always known at some point I'd have to deal with you and the adult decisions that you *think* you're ready to make while you're still just a child." My mother got up and walked over to the refrigerator and opened it. She reached inside and pulled out a bottled water. She opened it up, took a sip and said, "You've planned out your entire life and you know exactly what is in store for you, right?" My mother awaited my response.

"Yeah," I boldly declared, because I knew for certain that I wanted to marry Misalo, have four children, live in a beautiful house and have the perfect life. "I want to be like you and Dad. Misalo will be the perfect father and husband."

"So, if I were to tell you that he's only interested and fascinated with the diamond at the meeting of your thighs, you'd say—"

I glanced down at my thighs trying to figure out what she meant, then I suddenly got it.

"Misalo isn't like that, Mom. He's very special and nothing like boys were when you were young. He doesn't want to have sex with every girl in town."

"If he's that honorable, why doesn't he come to the front door like a respectable young man, instead of having you creep around like some tramp?" My mother placed her right index finger up to her temple. She looked at me sternly as if she wasn't going to believe a word I said and was clearly judging me and what her next move was going to be.

"I am not a tramp. Misalo *is* going to marry me one day, probably as soon as we graduate," I said, refusing to concede defeat to the battle of wits I was having with my mother.

"Do you know that for sure? Are you absolutely convinced that at the age of eighteen with his entire life ahead of him, he's going to trade in all of his freedom for a job, four children and a mountain of debt? The same question applies to you, Maya. Are you going to be willing to find a place to live, buy furniture, pay rent, get pregnant and sit at home all day with four babies who cry all of the time? Are you willing to stop shopping for the latest designer fashions that you love to wear and trade them in for clothes out of Walmart? Are you emotionally ready to deal with the possibility that he may grow tired of you and want his freedom back? Can you handle it if the fairy-tale love story you've concocted in your mind turns into a nightmare?"

Admittedly, I had not considered any of the things my mother was bringing up. All I knew was that love conquered all, and Misalo could do no wrong and he'd never do anything to hurt me. "Misalo and I are soul mates. I've read articles that have said once you find your soul mate nothing can tear you apart." My mother laughed and it really upset me. I was being serious and she thought I was joking.

"Why won't you give him a real chance? Why don't you think I know how to make good decisions when it comes to my love life?" I knew I was really pressing my luck with that comment, but I just couldn't allow my mother to have this victory.

"Misalo seemed like a nice enough boy when he took you to prom, but his behavior lately doesn't reflect well on him. He's still just a boy, Maya. He is nowhere near being the successful man that he has the potential to be. Strapping him down with your fantasy of marriage and children at such a young age will only make him resent you."

"You're wrong, Mom. Misalo wants the same things I do." I raised my voice as I felt my emotions getting away from me. My mother was making sense, but I didn't want to hear her words. Loving Misalo was my choice. I wanted to prove her wrong. I wanted to show her that I was right.

My mother moved closer to me and met my gaze. "I'm your mother, and I know you better than you know yourself. You know that I'm right and you're not going to win this argument."

"I am right!" I said with fire in my voice. I refused to break eye contact with her as I held my ground.

My mother snappily replied, "You can't hide those lying eyes of yours, Maya. You know you're not right. You can lie to yourself your entire life, but honey, one thing you'll never be able to do is lie to your mother."

I remained silent as a few tears surfaced and spilled over. Humiliated, I quickly smeared them away from both of my cheeks. My breathing became sporadic. I was trying to keep from having a total emotional breakdown in front of her.

"I see that I'm going to have to save you from yourself." My mother turned her back to me, walked over to the kitchen window and looked out of it. "Your father is home."

I turned and looked in the same direction. I saw my father pulling his car into the garage.

"What do you think love is, Maya?"

I thought about her question before I answered with a trembling voice. "Love is when two people can't see living without each other. Love makes you miss them whenever they're not around and love makes you think about the person all of the time." I felt that I'd provided her with a reasonable and truthful answer.

"You're not in love. You're infatuated." It was clear she didn't like the answer I gave.

"Isn't passion part of being in love?" I asked.

"Yes, it is, but love is about so much more." My mother paused in thought. "Do you want to become a teen mom and turn your father and me into grandparents?"

"No," I quickly responded.

"But you want to have four children?" My mother threw my own words back at me.

"Well, not right away," I said.

"Maya, do you realize all types of sexually transmitted diseases are out there that you can get? Some have a cure and others don't."

"I know that, Mom, but it's not like that." By the pitch of her voice I could tell she was growing angrier.

"Oh, really? Then what is it like, Maya? Please enlighten

me. Explain to me why you'd purposely break the trust that your father and I have in you?"

"I didn't think about that, okay? I just wanted to see Misalo and spend time with him." I admitted more than I had wanted to.

Dad walked into the kitchen and heard every word I'd just said. Our eyes met and in his I could see a mixture of pain and disappointment. He didn't have to say a single word to me; his eyes were speaking for him. I felt as if I'd wounded him in the gravest of ways. The tears I'd been desperately trying to contain swelled in my eyes. I felt as if he thought I was no longer his innocent baby girl.

"Do you hear yourself, Maya? You were hanging out with this boy and came home with a broken leg!" my mother barked, then threaded her fingers through her hair. She looked at my father and said, "I've got this one. Anna is in her room. Please go talk to her." Without getting involved in the conversation I was having with my mother, Dad left to go deal with Anna.

"He didn't break my leg. It was an accident. How many times do I have to explain that?" I raised my voice, suddenly feeling incredibly crappy. I didn't want to hurt my dad. Somehow his pain transferred over to me and I felt his heartbreak. I tried to hold on to the emotional swell, but I couldn't. It was too powerful, like a tsunami. My head slumped and I burst into tears.

My mother pulled out the chair next to me and sat down. "You listen to me and you listen good. I don't want you near Misalo. You need to end your relationship with him, Maya."

"Are you serious?" I stood and walked over to the countertop and removed a few paper towel sheets to blow my nose. Once I'd cleaned myself up a little I sat back down.

"I'm certainly not playing around."

"I don't think I can do that," I said, crying uncontrollably once again.

"Sure you can. You just need a little time away from him. I think spending some time with your grandmother will help you get over him. Plus, now is the perfect time. She'll love the idea of you coming to visit for a little while."

"Oh, God!" I groaned before burying my face in the palms of my hands. At that moment I would have preferred to run into a burning building than be trapped with my quirky grandmother.

My mother walked over to the countertop where she'd placed her purse when she'd walked in. She opened it and searched for her cell phone. "I'm going to give your grandmother a call. You can go to your room now, and don't come out unless I call for you."

I excused myself and ran upstairs to my bedroom. I walked past Anna's room and saw her crying a bucket of tears, as well. Whatever our father said to her didn't make her feel good at all. I wanted to slam my door shut, but knew that I'd only extend an invitation for my father to come in, so I didn't.

I thought I'd at least have a few days before my mother shipped me off for an extended stay with my grandmother, but I was wrong. As soon as my mother got off the phone with her, she came into my bedroom and told me to pack because I'd be leaving first thing in the morning.

"What about Anna? Is she being forced to go, as well?" I asked, hoping to drag her along with me.

"No. She is not going with you," my mother said curtly. It wasn't the answer I'd hoped for.

"Well, I have to do some laundry. Can I come out of my room to do that?" I asked, surrendering to the fact that my mother had won.

"Yes," my mother answered as she shut my door. I wanted to scream, but knew that would only get me into deeper trouble. The sound of my phone buzzing on my bed caught my attention. I thought it was Misalo calling, and I couldn't wait to share with him the horrible news of my departure. When I picked up the phone I noticed the incoming call was from Keysha.

"Hello," I answered tearfully.

"What's wrong with you? Why do you sound like you just took a pregnancy test that came back positive?" Keysha immediately picked up on the sorrow in my voice.

"Ha, ha, very funny. I got busted today," I answered.

"For real?" Keysha asked.

"Yeah, thanks to my sister."

"Anna? What did she do?"

"She was born. That's what she did."

"Okay, besides being born, how did she wreck your afternoon with Misalo?" Keysha asked. I laid it all out to her and she couldn't believe how low-down my little sister was.

"I'm sorry, but what Anna did was inexcusable. My brother, Mike, and I barely get along most of the time, but he'd never throw me under a bus the way your sister did you. Why is she like that?"

"I think she was dropped on her head or something as a baby. That girl has mental issues."

"Why can't your parents just ground you for a few days or something? Why go to the extreme of sending you to live with your grandmother?"

"I don't know. This was my mother's grand idea," I said, utterly exasperated.

"So, what are you going to do now?" Keysha asked.

"I really don't have a choice in the matter," I said glumly.

"Well, where does your grandmother live? Maybe I can come visit you or something. Is your grandmother going to keep you under lock and key?"

"She lives in Pilsen on the lower west side of Chicago. Not too far from the University of Chicago."

"Okay, I know where the University of Chicago is. I'd have to take a bus to the Metra train station and then take a train downtown to Roosevelt Road. Then I'd have to catch a bus over to the Pilsen area."

"Keysha, that sounds like a lot of traveling. Heck, by the time you reach me half of the day will be gone. Besides, my grandmother isn't going to let me out of her sight. She thinks everyone in the world has gone crazy," I grumbled.

"There isn't even a slight chance that we'll get a chance to hang out?" Keysha was still hoping.

"I don't know. When I get there I'll have to let you know. It's been a while since I've spent some time with my grandmother, and I have a feeling that she's going to want to spend every waking moment of the day with me."

"Wow, that sucks. Have you spoken to Misalo? Does he know what's gone down?"

"No, not yet." I sighed loudly. "Oh, I almost forgot to mention that my mother and my father don't want me to see Misalo anymore. They want me to break up with him."

"No way! Are you serious? Why?" Keysha seemed more upset about that one than I was.

"They believe Misalo is bad news and blah, blah, blah. But I don't care what they say. I'm still going to see him. There is no way I'm going to let my folks rip us apart."

"Wow, Maya. I never thought your parents would turn on you like that. I thought they liked Misalo."

"They did, but now they don't," I said, getting angry about it all over again.

"So, how are you going to continue to see him?" Keysha asked.

"I don't know. I haven't figured that one out yet, but I do know one thing—my parents can't be with me all the time, so whenever I do see him again we'll have to make the best use of our time," I said, thinking about a way to slip away from my grandmother's house to meet up with Misalo somewhere in the city.

"Enough about my drama. Just thinking about what's in store for me is giving me a headache. So, what's up with you and that guy who came to the swimming pool? Did you get his number?" I asked, figuring that was one of the reasons for her phone call.

"You're talking about Cocky Carlo. Nah, there was no love connection there. He just moved into the neighborhood. He seems okay, but as far as the attraction thing goes, I just wasn't feeling him. Besides, there was something about his eyes. He looked at me as if he was trying to hypnotize me or something. It was really strange. I felt as if I could see what he was thinking."

"And what was he thinking?" I asked.

"About how to have sex with me," Keysha answered.

"I think you're just being cautious because of all the stuff you went through with Wesley, Antonio and Jerry," I said, playing the role of psychoanalyst.

"I don't know. The lack of my attraction to him may be something a little deeper," Keysha said cautiously.

"Wait a minute. Why did you say it like that? Something is up. Come on, spill it. What's going on?" I asked.

"Okay, I know this is going to sound crazier than a Lady Gaga outfit, but I sort of miss Wesley."

"Oh, Lord, Keysha that does sound crazy," I said, over-exaggerating my words.

"I know, but I can't help it. I don't know why my heart has decided to do a 180-degree turn on me."

"Have you been talking to him again?" I asked.

"No comment," Keysha said.

"OMG! What have you guys been talking about? How could you keep this from me?" I asked, slightly upset.

"It's nothing, really. I've only spoken to him like three times. We were just talking about general stuff, but I liked having a conversation with him. He's even started writing his poetry again and shared a few of them with me. They were really good poems. I suggested he submit them for prize money, or try to attend a poetry slam, or even get on that show called *Brave New Voices*. Lord knows he's been through enough to write a really good socially conscious spoken-word piece."

"Wesley sounds like he is the one who really makes you happy," I said.

"He's just a friend, that's all." I knew she wasn't ready to admit that she still had a thing for him, but I wasn't about to push the issue.

"Girl, let me call you back. My head is starting to kill me, and I still have to do laundry and pack," I said, wanting to end the conversation.

"Okay. Call me when you feel better," Keysha said.

"I will. I'm just a little depressed right now," I admitted.

"Well, if there is anything I can do, just let me know," Keysha offered.

"I will. TTYL," I said before hanging up.

# nine

VIVIANA

I awoke to the sound of my mother and Martin having an argument. I didn't know if they had come home late last night while I was asleep or first thing this morning. What I did know was that he sounded like a grizzly bear howling in the wilderness. From what I could gather, he was angry with her because some other guy in his motorcycle club had started flirting with her and she appeared to enjoy it. My mother was just as angry, speaking to him in rapid Spanglish, which is a mixture of Spanish and English languages. That was a sure sign that she was just as ticked off. As always, I felt a deep need to be my mother's backup in case Martin decided to get physical with her. Reaching underneath my pillow, I grabbed the knife. I placed my bare feet on the cold floor and walked over to the door. Before I opened it, I pulled the drawstring tighter on my turquoise shorts that I'd slept in and knotted it. I stepped out into the hall and noticed their bedroom door was slightly ajar. Taking a deep breath, I approached the door, pushing it open a little farther, and saw that Martin had ahold of my mother by the wrists. He looked like a giant towering over her.

"You belong to me. You need to remember that. If you even dream about being with another man you'll regret it." Martin shook my mother violently.

My mother fought back as best as she could and said, "Well then, you need to tell your ex, Novia, to stay away from you. I'm tired of your ex-girlfriend smiling at you like she wants to make secret plans with you. Are you still dealing with her?"

Martin shook her violently once again. "I'm not dealing with anyone but you. But I think you're trying to creep around on me. That's what my boys are saying. They told me that you were going around—"

"Let her go, or else," I said as I tightened my grip on the knife, which I kept concealed from his view.

"Oh, you want some of this, too, little señorita!" Martin's eyes were bloodred and filled with rage. He was so angry I wouldn't be surprised to see steam coming out of his nose.

"I'm working on saving up enough money so I can get me and my mother out of here and into our own place. We don't need you!" I bravely stood up to him.

"Did you hear her?" Martin looked at my mother, then let her go. He started walking toward me. I once again tightened the grip on the blade, ready to plunge it deep into his neck if he so much as lifted a hand to me. "What you don't understand, little girl, is that your mother belongs to me. I own her. And since you're part of her, I own you as well, and if I—"

"Baby, look at me. I'm sorry. You were so right. I should

have told you the moment that guy started bothering me."
My mother stood in his path and prevented him from reaching me. Martin turned his attention back to my mother.

My mother glanced over her shoulder at me. Black lines of mascara ran like railroad tracks down her cheeks. Her eyes were just as red and glassy as his. "Viviana, it's okay, honey. This is what all couples who love each other do. Fighting is just a natural part of being loved."

I gazed at my mother, completely perplexed by what she was saying.

"Go on back to your room, or better yet, go visit your new little friend downstairs. And stop all of that nonsense talk of us getting our own place. We don't need one, because Martin is providing us with all we need."

My jaw dropped when my mother said that to me. I didn't understand how she could possibly want to live in Martin's grubby apartment. At that moment I thought maybe she was considering marrying him.

"Are you going to marry him?" I asked.

"Viviana!" My mother gave me an evil look that said that was the wrong question to ask.

"Maybe I should marry you and turn you into a respectable woman instead of a—"

I interrupted Martin. "What about my father, Salena? Don't you miss him at all?" I snapped. My mother knew that I was equally ticked off because I called her by her first name.

"Ain't no logic in loving a dead man, little girl." Martin found the love of my father to be something to laugh at. "As far as I could tell your daddy was a real—"

"Be careful of what you say!" I snarled.

"Oh, are you threatening me?" Martin tried once again to reach me, but my mother blocked him.

"No, no," she said, pressing the palm of her hand against his mighty chest. I waited for my mother to say something that would make Martin honor my father, but she didn't. She just continued to plead with her eyes for me to leave, but I refused.

Finally she said, "I'll be okay. Martin and I just had a little too much to drink, isn't that right?" My mother flipped the script and was now lovingly caressing his brown cheek.

"I can hold my liquor. Now, the stuff I was smoking, well, that's a different story." He glanced down at my mother, fire still in his eyes.

"Run along now, Viviana. I know how to make my big strong hombre feel better." Now my mother had flipped the script yet again by speaking the mixed language in a loving way instead of an angry one. I stood frozen and confused. I didn't know what to think. My mind was swirling. Anger, fear, revenge and contempt were all competing for control of my next move.

"Go!" my mother said, as Martin's hands began gliding up and down her spine.

I didn't know if they were in love or hated each other's guts. The only things I knew for sure was that he wasn't my father and I didn't trust him any more than I'd trust a drug addict in a room filled with dope. And my mother, well, she still believed that her love was strong enough to save men who had hearts of stone. My mother eased her way over to the door, and I stepped out of the room. I was looking back at her when she slammed the door shut. Bewildered, I turned around and walked back to my grimy bedroom.

Later that morning I got a text from Toya telling me to meet her outside in front of the building. I was dying to get out of the house. It didn't take me long to get dressed. As I walked out of my room I heard the stereo in Martin's room blaring loudly. It was playing some old song "Always and Forever" by a group called Heat Wave. The only reason I knew the song was because I'd once caught an episode of the George Lopez show, and George was doing his stand-up comedy and he'd mentioned the song and the group.

Utterly disgusted with my mom, I grabbed my duffel bag to place my stolen merchandise in and rushed out the door without so much as leaving a note on the refrigerator door as to where I was going and when I'd be back. My mother couldn't have cared less either way. When I saw Toya, she was standing on the driver's side of a black Camaro lip-locked with some guy. Once their kissing session was over, the dude got in the car and drove off.

"Who was that?" I asked.

"My baby daddy," Toya proudly said. "He came to pick up his son. Are you ready to hop on the bus and head downtown to do this?"

"Yeah, but couldn't he have like, given us a ride?" I asked, thinking that if he had a car as nice as a Camaro, why wouldn't he have given us a ride?

"He doesn't have time right now. He has to go and handle his business," Toya explained. I was about to question what business he was going to handle with a baby, but decided that it wasn't worth starting an argument.

"Come on," I said and started heading toward the bus stop.

"My, aren't you eager today," she said, noticing my brisk pace.

"I need to make some money so I can get the hell out of that apartment with my mother's boyfriend. He's a real—"

Toya finished my sentence for me. "Jackass?"

"That and a bunch more," I said.

"What do you think about you and me getting an apartment together?" Toya asked.

"How are we going to do that? You live with your blind grandmother," I reminded her.

"She's been talking about going into a senior citizen apartment building lately. It's not like I want to live with her forever. Besides, she has too many rules. Not that I follow them, but sometimes it gets on my nerves."

"I'd love to get an apartment with you and be your roommate, but how are we going to pull that one off? We're too young to sign a lease and we don't have jobs. The best I can hope for is to convince my mother to leave that idiot."

"Girl, we live in the 'hood. I know plenty of shady landlords who only care about one thing, and that's getting paid. As long as we can come up with the rent, we're cool."

"And if we don't?" I asked.

"Then we just negotiate some new terms with the landlord, that's all." Toya smiled confidently. I glanced at her for a moment, but said nothing.

"I'll think about it," I said, not wanting to make any type of real commitment to that plan, because in spite of everything wrong in my life, I couldn't stand the thought of being without my mother. I'd already lost my father, and to lose my mother as well would make me go even crazier.

During the bus ride downtown, Toya and I mapped out the places we'd hit. The Illinois State building in downtown Chicago had a massive food court and there were always tons of people there. We also agreed to hit all of the commuter train stations, as well as the Amtrak train station. It would be really easy to pick someone's pocket there, because people had a tendency to fall asleep while waiting for their train.

"I just had another brilliant idea." Toya leaned in closer to me.

"What is it?" I asked curiously.

"I don't know why I hadn't thought of this before." Toya thumped her forehead with the heel of her hand. "Airports," she whispered.

"Huh?" I asked, confused.

"Viviana, we could hang around the baggage terminals at the airport." I gave Toya a quizzical look, and I could see her idea was still developing in her mind.

"Think about it. A lot of luggage looks alike. We could walk in, grab some luggage and walk right out the door and no one would even question us," Toya said.

"Why would I want someone else's funky clothes?" I was totally grossed out by the idea.

"It's not the clothes we're after. Well, not unless someone has some nice designer stuff." Toya made a funny gesture with her hand. "It's the other stuff that people put in their luggage, like cameras, jewelry, computers and other gifts that they may have picked up while on vacation."

"I thought people had those little locks they put on lug-

gage. We wouldn't be able to even open it up," I said, thinking that her idea wasn't a very good one. But Toya had an
answer for me that I didn't expect.

"No. I heard on the news that people can't lock their luggage up anymore. It's one of those Homeland Security re-
quirements."

"Okay. Say that we can get the luggage open. We don't
have X-ray vision. How are we going to know which piece
of baggage to walk off with? And what about all of the video
cameras they have in airports?"

"Oh, those are good questions. I hadn't thought about that
stuff," Toya conceded.

"See there. Besides O'Hare Airport is so far away from
where we live," I said.

"Yeah, but Midway Airport isn't. Look, we'd just have to
take our chances. We could have on hats or dark sunglasses
to hide our eyes and face." I could see that Toya wasn't giving
up, and the dangerousness of her idea was actually exciting
to her. That was something I'd noticed about her. Stealing,
to her, had no boundaries and the exhilaration of it all was
like a drug high. I, on the other hand, was just doing it as a
way to get money so that I could move on. I figured that if
I could save up about three or four thousand dollars, I'd be
able to find a little place for my mom, and still have enough
rent money to last for a little while. My mom could work
on getting another job, and I could find a little part-time
job doing something. I really didn't care what type of job it
was, just as long as it was legal and the pay was steady. First,
I had to get the money and, according to Toya, on a good
day she could easily pull in a thousand dollars. So I figured

if we did six or seven hits, I'd have the money in no time at all.

"I think we should at least give the airport thing a shot. We can hit the places downtown, and once we're done we can catch the El train out to Midway Airport," Toya said.

"Okay," I said, but in the back of my mind, I still thought it was a lame idea.

As the bus drove past the McCormick Place convention center, both Toya and I noticed there was some huge conference going on.

"What do you think about hitting a big meeting like that?" I asked, watching wave after wave of people walking into the building.

"I don't know. I've never tried to hit a place like this. Besides, it looks like all of these people are dressed in business clothes and I don't have any outfits like that, that would help me blend in."

I looked back at Toya and chuckled. "Well, when we take some of the luggage from the airport, let's hope you find one filled with business clothes that are your size."

Toya laughed. "Yeah, right, I don't want to wear someone else's funky clothes."

"Now you see what I mean," I said as I continued to laugh.

Toya and I arrived downtown and went to the Illinois State building first. Once there, we split up and agreed to meet one block away in about an hour. I walked around hoping some woman would leave her purse draped over the back of her chair, but that type of scenario never appeared. After seeing that I wasn't going to get lucky I decided to leave. However, before I did that I noticed that one level up from the food court there were a bunch of shops. I decided to kill time browsing. I looked at some pretty outfits that I couldn't afford, expensive jewelry, fashion accessories, fabrics and other items that I longed to have.

I finally met up with Toya as planned and was anticipating that, just like me, she'd had no luck.

"How much do you think you pulled in?" Toya asked.

"Nothing, no one left their purse on the back of their chair," I said.

"Are you kidding me?" Toya looked at me as if she was ticked off.

"What?" I asked, baffled.

"Viviana, I've taught you better than that. Why didn't you just find a mark and pick their pocket?"

"Because I didn't see any. There were mostly old and sickly looking people there," I said.

"Duh! They're the ones with the money," Toya said angrily.

"Don't tell me you ripped off the elderly," I said, feeling that old people were off-limits. As much as I wanted to do what Toya did and be as good as she was, I just couldn't see myself taking money from old people.

"Damn right I did, and I made four hundred dollars," Toya proudly boasted. We walked toward the Amtrak train station. "Look, girl. If you're going to hang with me you've got to be willing to do whatever it takes. I'm starting to think that you're not cut out for this. You're starting to make me think that you're just full of it!" Toya raised her voice at me and I didn't like it.

"So, what are you saying?" I stopped walking and decided to address the situation right then and there.

"What I'm saying is that you need to stop acting like a frightened dog in a thunderstorm. You need to step up to the freaking plate and take some swings."

"I'm not afraid," I said.

"I don't know. I think ever since that beat down you took on the bus, you've gotten cold feet." Toya sneered.

"I don't believe you just said that to me."

"Hey, I'm just calling it like I see it."

"Well, you need to get your damn vision checked!"

"Then prove me wrong. When we get to the train station, I'm going to pick someone out that you should be able to get. If you don't do it, I'm going to beat you down for wasting my damn time!" Toya swerved her head from right to left disapprovingly.

"Whatever! You don't scare me, Toya," I snarled, and walked ahead of her.

When Toya and I arrived at the Amtrak train station it was crowded with people who were waiting on the train. Some of them were asleep on seats with their luggage next to them, others were just standing around. Toya and I stood in a corner and took everything in.

"Look, right over there." Toya quickly pointed.

"What?" I asked.

"The white girl holding the baby in her lap," Toya said.

"She's just holding her sleeping baby," I said, noticing the baby appeared to be between the ages of one and two years old.

"She's about to make her move on the guy sleeping next to her," Toya said.

"No, she isn't. How do you know that? The guy is probably her father or something."

"Just watch. She's using that baby to block the view of everyone else." Sure enough, as we continued to watch, the young girl was able to slip her fingers inside the man's pocket and remove money. She was also able to slip off his watch.

"Oh, she's damn good," Toya said, admiring the girl's work. Once the girl was done, she dropped the items into a nearby diaper bag and then moved away.

"See, Viviana, that's what I'm talking about. I can respect a girl like that. She's freaking fearless!" Toya became excited by what we'd both just witnessed. "Oh, wait a minute. I just spotted a perfect one. You see the guy over at the ticket booth." Toya pointed the man out.

"Yeah, I see him," I said, noticing he was a handsome Asian man wearing a black business suit.

"He's going to put his wallet in the inside pocket of his suit jacket," Toya said.

"How do you know that?"

"Because I just saw him take it out of it." We both watched as the man pulled out a money clip full of cash to pay for his ticket.

"Oh, yeah," Toya whispered, "and he is carrying a wad of cash." A vile smile formed on her face.

"I'm going to get this one. I want you to watch and pay close attention. Then I'm going to pick out someone for you. Obviously, the pickings here are pretty good if the white chick is hanging out and making her rounds." Toya was in

the zone and nothing was going to keep her from victimiz-
ing the man at the ticket booth. I scanned the room for the
location of the white girl and noticed her watching the same
guy.

"Hey, I think—"

"Shhh," Toya silenced me. "Just watch me work." Toya
moved away from me and approached the man. Someone
had left a copy of a newspaper on a seat and Toya picked it
up. The newspaper would conceal her hand when she slipped
it inside the man's pocket. From my point of view I noticed
that the white chick holding the baby had spotted Toya. I
don't know how thieves can spot each other, but the white
girl definitely knew Toya was going after the Asian guy.

"I think the white girl wants the same target Toya is after,"
I mumbled to myself. I was about to warn Toya, but she'd
gotten across the room rather quickly and was now standing
directly behind the Asian man. As soon as he turned around
he'd have no choice but to bump into her. I looked around
again for the other thief in the room and noticed that she
was talking to a police officer who had a black-and-brown
German shepherd with him.

"Oh, my God!" I whispered. "She's pointing Toya out to
the police." I suddenly felt as if I were watching a movie.
The cop focused in on Toya. The Asian man turned around
and bumped into her, and with lightning-quick fingers Toya
had slipped inside the man's suit pocket, lifted his wallet and
hid it within the fold of the newspaper she was carrying. By
the time the Asian man apologized for bumping into Toya,
the cop and the K-9 were standing next to them. The police
officer asked the man if he had any identification on him.

The poor man reached for his wallet and realized that it was missing. Toya, as swiftly as she could, turned and tried to get away.

"Excuse me, miss." The cop tried to get her attention. Toya ignored him and kept moving, but in a panic started running. The cop unleashed the German shepherd, which immediately cornered her.

"Come get this dog!" Toya screamed as he continued to bark viciously at her. Toya coiled up the newspaper and raised her hand to swing at the dog. No sooner had her hand gone into the air, than the man's wallet came flying out. Busted.

I turned to search for the thief who'd snitched, but she had disappeared.

"Viviana!" Toya screamed as the cop spun her around and pressed her face against one of the walls.

"Oh, crap!" I mumbled. I was nervous and didn't know whether I should go to her or just take off. I decided to take off. I turned my back on Toya as she repeatedly called my name. I had no idea how she thought I'd be of any help. In my hastiness to get away I turned a corner and nearly tripped over the other thief. She was with a guy, who was holding the baby.

"This will be the only warning you'll get," said the girl, who leaned in close to me and purposely spoke into my ear. "Don't ever come back to this side of town trying to take my money, or you'll end up in jail just like your friend." I stood still, frozen like a statue. My mind was still trying to process everything that had just happened.

"If I were you I'd leave now," said the girl.

I continued on my way and never once looked back.

# ten

*MAYA*

AS my grandmother Esmeralda drove me back to her house she mentioned how overjoyed she was about my visiting her for a little while. Spending more time with all of her grandchildren was very important to her. When I was a little girl I was always at her house listening to her drone on about stories and events that I didn't particularly care about at the time. She took me and my siblings to church on Sunday and often signed us up for activities there. She had me in everything from performing Mexican folk dances at the church to Bible study for children. However, when I turned thirteen and was able to have a little more say in how I spent my time, the first thing I wanted to do was stop hanging out with my grandmother and relax with my friends. Sunday afternoons at the mall replaced Sundays at church, and it was easy to get out of seeing her on Saturday because all I had to say was, "I've got homework to do," and that pretty much guaranteed that I didn't have to go visit. I wasn't lying a majority of the time. I did have homework to do, but not as much as I led my mother to believe. When I wasn't in school, I got out of spending time with my grandmother by attending summer school or getting involved in some other community activity near my home. Once I'd turned sixteen and was able to work, my job with Keysha at the swimming pool was another perfect reason to keep from visiting.

It's not that I don't like my grandmother. I really do love her, it's just that she is so old-fashioned and loves tradition. I've heard her and my mother more often than not fussing about why my mom doesn't come around very often. My mother would always point out how hectic things were at the office, and how tiring it was to raise three children. Of course my grandmother Esmeralda felt that there was always time for *familia*. Speaking of family, my grandmother had two movies that she could watch over and over again and never tire of. Those films were *My Family,* starring Jimmy Smits, Edward James Olmos and Esai Morales, and *Forrest Gump*. The movie *My Family* came out in 1995 when I was only a year old and *Forrest Gump* came out in 1994, the year I was born. I once asked Keysha if her grandmother or mother had a movie that they watched all of the time.

"I don't know about my grandmother Rubylee," Keysha had said. "But my mother, Justine, watched *Purple Rain* to the point that she knew all of the actors' lines." I remembered laughing at that.

My grandmother Esmeralda wasn't a very tall woman, but she wasn't too short, either. She had long black hair that cascaded down her back, and skin as soft as rose petals. Deeper and more pronounced age lines had formed around her eyes, nose and lips since I'd last seen her. Her wisdom lines made her appear a little more Native American than

Mexican American. She was sixty-three and for the most part had stayed in decent shape. Although, my mother told me, after my grandfather's sudden passing it took a long time for Grandmother Esmeralda to get over his death, and she ended up losing too much weight. My grandfather passed away when I was just two years old, so I don't really remember him. I do recall hearing stories about him, but it had been so long that I didn't really remember any of them.

"Did you know that your grandfather was as handsome as Jimmy Smits?" asked my grandmother as we exited the highway. I knew she wanted me to act as if I was unfamiliar with the actor, so she could bring up the movie *My Family*.

"Jimmy who?" I just played along with her.

"Jimmy Smits. Oh, let me tell you. Your grandfather was the best husband and father in the world. When I met him in the 1960s, all the girls in the neighborhood were after him. They would do such silly things to get his attention. They'd walk past him when he came out onto the front porch of his home and blow kisses at him. When I'd see him at our high school dances, all of my girlfriends would argue over who was going to make him their guy. My friends and I were only sophomores at the time and he was a junior. So for us to be able to snag an upperclassman was big stuff." I knew I'd heard this story before, but for some reason I was so much more interested in it now than I'd ever been before.

"So, how did you get him?" I asked, because I truly didn't remember.

"Oh, come on, Maya. I know I've told you this story a thousand times, at least." Grandmother Esmeralda smiled.

The deep lines around the corners of her eyes were really pronounced when she smiled.

"Well, you need to tell it to me one thousand and one times," I said.

"Well, while all of my girlfriends were busy chasing him, I completely ignored him," she explained. "It wasn't like I was ugly or anything, and in fact I had plenty of young fellas interested in dating me. But my father and your great-grandfather was very, very strict. There was no way that his daughter was going to get mixed up with some smooth-talking boy." Grandmother Esmeralda laughed before she continued on with her story. "Anyway, when I was in my third year of high school and your grandfather was in his last year, he started paying attention to me. He tried to make me swoon with his pretty hair and dreamy eyes, but I fought him off. But believe me, it wasn't easy."

"So why did you hold back? Why didn't you just go for it? I've always heard that the 1960s were when kids were saying stuff like, 'Make love and don't drop bombs,'" I said.

"True, there were a lot of things going on, but I respected my father. There was no way that I was going to go against his wishes. I was a good Catholic girl," she explained.

"I'm so glad I wasn't dating back then. I would've just died," I said jokingly.

"You would've survived just fine. You'd have good morals and values," Grandmother Esmeralda said. In the back of my mind I was like, *Whatever!* I thought she was done telling her story, but she continued.

"So I ignored him as much as I could. Then he graduated from high school and I was heartbroken."

"Heartbroken?" I laughed. "You weren't even dating the guy," I said, wondering how she could've been so upset.

"He and I had our moments, Maya," she whispered.

"What?" I asked because I didn't hear her.

"We held hands and kissed a few times, in secret, of course," she reluctantly admitted.

"So you *did* go against your father?" I asked, looking for clarification.

"Holding someone's hand and kissing them under a tree in the park is hardly criminal," she said, downplaying those early intimate moments. My intuition told me that much more than a kiss and a hug happened between them, but I wasn't about to go there with my grandmother.

"Okay, so there was some type of spark between you two," I said.

"Yes there was, and when he graduated I felt as if my world had fallen apart. I cried for days."

"Why? He still lived in the neighborhood, right?" I asked.

"No. You really don't remember me telling you this story, do you?" She glanced over at me just before she made another turn.

"No, I don't."

"Your grandfather was drafted into the army and sent off to the war in Vietnam in 1965."

"Oh, yeah, I forgot about that," I said, recalling several old photos I'd seen of him in uniform.

"He asked me to write to him and I did. I wrote him letters every day when he was in training at a military base in North Carolina. He'd write back just as often telling me that the training was actually sort of fun and that he was looking forward to serving his country. He was eighteen and young. He didn't really know what he was in for, and neither did the other men. When they shipped him off to Vietnam I didn't get a letter from him until he'd arrived over there. He asked me to send a photo of myself so he could think about me when all hell was breaking loose. By that point he hadn't seen any combat yet and his letters were still rather cheery and upbeat. However, here at home all we saw were horrible images from the war. I sent him a nice picture and my crucifix, which I got from the priest at Our Lady of Guadalupe Church when I was a little girl. The priest had blessed it and told me it would protect me always. I felt that it would help protect your grandfather, Miguel, so I sent it to him."

"Was it this one?" I asked, noticing the crucifix dangling from her rearview mirror.

"No. I buried it with your grandfather." Grandmother Esmeralda's voice trailed off, and I knew immediately that even after all of the years that had come to pass she still missed my grandfather.

"You don't have to talk about this anymore if you don't want to," I said, offering her a way out of the conversation.

"No. I need to tell you these stories as many times as necessary so that you remember them. It is the history of your family and it is very important and you must never forget it. Think about it, Maya. Had your grandfather not survived that war, your mother would've never been born and you wouldn't be sitting here with me."

I took a hard swallow. I hadn't thought about it like that.

"I received a letter from him one day and, anyway, in one

of his letters he told me when he returned he wanted to get married and settle down."

"How romantic," I said as I allowed myself to get completely lost in the story.

"Oh, Maya, my dear child, just listen to me. It is true—getting letters in the mail from your grandfather had a certain romantic touch. In fact, as soon as a letter would arrive I'd rush up to my bedroom, shut the door and read it. I truly fell in love with him through the letters he wrote."

"What did he say in them?" I asked.

"He talked about some of everything. His childhood, his deepest feelings, his hopes, his dreams. You name it. At least that's what he wrote about in the beginning, but the longer he stayed the more convinced he became that America wasn't doing anyone any good."

"Why? From what I've learned in my history classes, whenever America goes to war the history books say that we're justified."

"That's the problem with history books. You don't get to talk to the people who lived through it." My grandmother sighed. "Miguel hated being over there because he had to go from village to village burning down the homes of people who were very poor. He said to me in one of his letters,

Esmeralda, you should see the sad look in their eyes. They've lost all hope. They're mostly simple farmers who have homes made out of grass and mud. I've seen and done horrible things. It is as if hell has risen up from beneath the earth and has chosen to go on a killing spree.

"When I think about those letters and those times, I get sad."

"Wow," I said solemnly.

"One letter in particular really made me angry and I loved him, all at the same time. He said,

My Dear Esmeralda, Today I cried like a motherless child. My unit had to go into a village after an air strike and saw horrible things. I saw things that I can't even put into words, but I will do my best to try to tell you why I am so incredibly heartbroken. Today I saw a little Vietnamese girl who was about nine years old. The skin on her torso had melted off from the heat of the explosions. She was running down the road toward me wearing only her underwear. Other men in my unit acted as if they didn't see the child. I guess it's the training we go through. We're not supposed to really get too involved. Our job is to find the enemy and take them out. But this little girl was frightened by everything that was going on. The only thing she wanted to do was flee from the noise. Something in my heart shattered when I saw her. I put down my weapons and got on my knees and held my arms out to her. When she ran to me and wrapped her arms around my neck, she refused to let me go. Finally she just cried and I cried with her. This damn war doesn't care about innocent children. I feel as if I'm killing my own brothers and it's not right.

"Miguel carried the little girl to the medic and forced him to help her," Grandmother Esmeralda said.

"Oh, my God! What did you say to him after that?" I asked, feeling very sad.

"When I wrote him back I told him that he was a good man and would be a good father because of his caring heart. I also told him that I loved him and would be waiting for him whenever he came home." We finally arrived at Grandmother Esmeralda's gray-stone styled home. Her home was old, but similar in style to the one I'd seen on reruns of *The Cosby Show*.

"Come on, let's go inside and I'll tell you more over a glass of sun tea," said my grandmother. I gathered my belongings from the trunk and made my way up the concrete steps, through two sets of doors, and finally dropped my bags in the vestibule. To my immediate left there was a staircase that led to the upper level. To my right was the living room with a beautiful fireplace, and directly in front of me were the kitchen and the back porch.

"You can run those upstairs and place them inside your mother's old bedroom. I'll go pour us some tea. Come sit with me on the back porch when you're done."

About fifteen minutes later, I was sitting next to my grandmother, drinking some of the most delicious tea I'd ever tasted. She'd also sliced a piece of her upside-down pineapple cake on a small saucer for me.

"Oh, my God! I haven't had a slice of your pineapple cake in ages," I said, cutting into it with my fork. As soon as the morsel was in my mouth I felt my toes curling up.

"You should visit more often," she said, taking a sip of her tea.

"Okay, so what happened next?" I asked.

"I graduated from high school and got a job as a clerk for the city," she said.

"Where was Grandpa? Was he still at war?" I asked.

"Yes. He finally came home in the winter of 1967. He'd been wounded. He lost the lower half of his left leg. They gave him a prosthetic leg and physical therapy, and when he was well enough he was released."

"That sucks!" I said, looking down at my own leg and wondering what it would look like if half of it was missing.

"Yes, it did, but your grandfather was a very strong man. Even though he walked with a limp for the rest of his life, he didn't allow the loss of the leg to slow him down."

"So, were you happy to see him when he came back messed up like that?" I asked.

"Of course I was, although at first I didn't even know he was back home. You see, your grandfather arrived home during the worst blizzard in Chicago's history. Everything was shut down, sidewalks and roads were completely impassable. But your grandfather arrived in Chicago by train. It was snowing so hard people were told to stay indoors. Your grandfather didn't want to be stuck at the train station, so he convinced a cab driver to take him as far as he could. Your grandfather got within two miles of my house and walked the rest of the way."

"He walked two miles in a blizzard with one leg?" I asked for clarification.

"Yes, he did. He walked through over two feet of snow just to ring my doorbell. He didn't even stop to see his parents. He came to see me first. When my father, Don, answered the door, your grandfather Miguel was standing there dressed in his uniform, with his hat tucked under his arm and a green army bag filled with his belongings. He was covered from head to toe with snow. I was standing behind my father and heard him say, "Sir, my name is Miguel and I've just returned home from the war. Your daughter and I have been writing each other for a long time, and I'd like to know if it is okay with you if I were to sit and visit with her."

"Ohhh," I said, feeling my heart melt. "What happened then?"

"Well, my father didn't know what to make of his crazy stunt. He couldn't believe that Miguel had walked through a snowstorm just to see me. He respected Miguel's courage and the honorable way that he asked if he could spend time with me. It also helped that my father was a military man and understood how important it was to see people you cared about when you've been away for so long. He allowed Miguel in. My mother was in the middle of making tamales and asked Miguel to stay for dinner. He said he'd loved to, because he missed eating home-cooked meals. Miguel and I sat on the sofa and he unclasped the crucifix I'd sent to him. He placed it in my hand and said that it was truly blessed because he should've died, but he believed that it had protected him. I told him to keep it because I wanted it to protect him forever. And the rest, as they say, is history."

"So you didn't care about his leg being messed up?" I asked, thinking of how she might have been embarrassed to be seen with a guy who limped.

"Heavens no, child. When you truly love someone you see past things like that. I wasn't in love with the man's body. I was in love with what's right here." My grandmother placed her hand over my heart. I took a moment to think about what she'd said.

"So, then you started dating Grandpa?" I asked.

"Oh, yes. We dated for a year. We had so much fun together. I remember one time he came and asked my father if it was okay if he kept me out all night. I was almost twenty years old and he was still asking my father for permission, and my father loved him for it."

"Where did you guys go?" I cautiously asked, hoping that my question wasn't too personal.

"We went to see Carlos Santana. That was a great concert," she said, reminiscing on the moment.

"I actually like his music," I said.

"He is one of the best musicians in the world. I love Santana. I also loved your grandfather. We got married in 1968 and in 1969 your mother, Raven, was born. The following year in 1970, your aunt Salena was born. He loved his two girls and spoiled them rotten," she said, laughing.

Grandmother Esmeralda and I spent the rest of the day talking. When I was first told that I had to come visit her I thought for sure I'd be bored out of my mind, but I actually found visiting with her to be enjoyable. I don't know; maybe because I was a little older, but whatever the reason I was happy I'd come.

The following day Grandmother Esmeralda and I ran errands together. We rode around the Pilsen community visiting local shops that had been family-owned for generations. We visited a bookstore, a grocery store that made fresh tortillas, and even took time to visit the National Museum of Mexican Art. I walked around looking at the artifacts, but to me they didn't mean much.

"Maya, do you remember any of our family history that I've told you about?" she asked as we causally glanced at a display that chronicled the Afro-Mexican slave trade.

"Not really," I said as I read something that caught my eye. "'In 1492 King Ferdinand and Queen Isabella expelled the Islamic Moors out of Spain and back to Africa and started the exploration of the new lands to expand their growing empire.' Hmm, I never knew that," I said.

"Knew what?" Esmeralda asked.

"That people from Africa lived in Spain."

"Yes, this is true," said Grandmother Esmeralda. "Spaniards brought slaves to Mexico as well as the United States. That is why some Mexicans have features that look more African than Aztec, but we are all from the same country, just different parts of it."

"So the Aztec Indians were in Mexico before the Spanish and the Africans got there," I said as more of a question than a statement.

"Yes. See, look right here. In 1519 a man named Hernán Cortés from Spain seized the Aztec capital of Tenochtitlan. There is so much history that you can learn in a place like this," Grandmother Esmeralda said.

"I see," I said as I continued on. I came across information about revolts due to the combined efforts of the Mexican and African people that I'd never known about. "They don't teach this stuff in my high school history class," I said.

"Of course not, this is the history of Mexico."

"But, Mexico was once the United States." I found myself engaging in an intellectual conversation with my grandmother. This was something that was really weird.

"Oh, honey, you can tell people that until you're blue, but people always downplay it as if it is something that should be forgotten. This is why I like to bring my grandchildren to places like this, so that you can learn. These are important things to know, but sadly many Mexican people don't understand their own history."

"But why?" I asked.

"For a lot of reasons," Grandmother Esmeralda said as we made our way out the door. We stepped into the sunshine and I reached into my purse and pulled out my sunglasses. The warm sun felt great against my skin, but it wouldn't be long before I got thirsty.

"Come on, let's walk this way," she said. I walked alongside her. By the time we made it back to her car, my entire back felt sticky with sweat.

"If feels like it's one hundred degrees out here today," Grandmother Esmeralda complained as she turned on the air conditioner.

"Tell me about it. I feel like I'm melting." We made a few more stops before we finally headed back home. After I took a shower and freshened up, I joined my grandmother in her bedroom. I know that I shouldn't have been surprised, but she'd popped in the movie *My Family* for us to watch.

"This is such a fantastic movie." She smiled at me.

"Uhm, don't you have cable? We could probably find another movie to watch," I suggested.

"I just have basic cable and nothing good is ever on. But

this movie here is excellent." As much as I didn't want to watch the film, I crawled into the bed beside her and watched it.

At some point I fell asleep and awoke later that evening to the sound of a blender. I took a long stretch and relaxed just a little longer. I then heard the faint sound of music echoing from the kitchen. I finally got up and walked toward the sound and realized that Grandmother Esmeralda was listening to a song called "Maria Maria" by Carlos Santana.

"What are you doing listening to that song?" I asked, completely surprised because I thought for sure the only music my grandmother liked was from the 1960s and '70s.

"Hey, once a Carlos Santana fan you're a fan for life." My grandmother did a little dance where she worked her hips. I almost had to slap myself because I couldn't believe my eyes.

"Okay," I said long and slowly. "Have you been drinking?"

"No." My grandmother seemed offended by the comment. She poured whatever she was mixing up in the blender through a strainer and into a bowl.

"What is that?" I asked.

"Gazpacho, and it's very delicious," she said and offered me a spoonful. I took a taste and loved it. "You like?"

"Yeah, that's very good," I said as she lifted up another spoonful to my mouth. "What's in it?"

"You mean to tell me that your mother has never made this for you guys?"

"No, not that I remember," I said.

"Well, that's what grandmothers are for. I'll teach you

how to make it," she said. "Go wash your hands and come on back."

While I learned how to make gazpacho, I listened to music with my grandmother. We then sat down at her kitchen table and she shared more of her knowledge with me.

"Did you know that our family left Mexico in 1914? Your great-great-grandfather Phil came from Aguascalientes, Mexico. He came across the border to El Paso, Texas. He had to pay five cents to enter into the United States."

"Really?" I said, not caring too much about it because I was busy eating.

"Yes, he left to find work. He was young and single. He got a job working in the sugar beet fields. It was hard labor, but something was better than nothing. By 1918 he married a woman named Aurora Gomez and had your great-grandfather Don. Aurora insisted that Don learn how to become more American. She pushed him to learn how to speak English and forget about the old Mexican ways. His father, Phil, didn't like this, but Aurora won. In 1941 Don was twenty-three years old and hated working in the fields. So he signed up for the military and went off to serve in World War II. He served both in Europe and the Pacific. When he came back he told his parents that he wasn't going to go back to doing fieldwork. Instead he came to Chicago and got a job working at the steel mill. He worked very hard and made much more money than a fieldworker. By 1946, Don had met and married Caroline Lopez. In 1948 I was born. My mother, Caroline, came from a family who believed in the American dream and way of life and wanted to make sure that I had every advantage possible."

"Do you have pictures?" I asked. Because now I was very interested in the story.

"I thought you'd never ask," she said. "Hang on, they're in a box under my bed." Grandmother Esmeralda got up to go retrieve the photos. As I waited, I heard the doorbell ring.

"Do you want me to get it?" I called out to my grandmother.

"Hang on. I don't know who it could be. I'm not expecting any company," she said as she entered into the kitchen again. The doorbell chimed once again. I followed her toward the front door.

"Hang on, I'm coming!" she yelled out. Grandmother Esmeralda peeped through the viewfinder and gasped. "Oh, my goodness!" she said as she hurriedly opened the door. When the door opened up, there stood my aunt Salena. Her face was bruised and swollen. Her lip was busted and the dark sunglasses she was wearing were clearly hiding more battle scars. Standing beside her was my cousin Viviana. Her hair was pulled back from her face and braided into a long ponytail. Viviana looked rough. Her lips were dry and chapped; her skin was filled with blemishes and pimples that stretched across her forehead and along her jawline. The white-and-red bumps looked disgusting, and I suppose my facial expression said things that my mouth wasn't brave enough to. I opened my mouth to try and speak, but words escaped me. My eyes darted back and forth between Salena and Viviana. I was trying to process what had happened to them. Finally, Viviana said, "Maya! Would you move out of the way!"

"Oh," I said, as I flinched before stepping aside to allow them to enter.

# eleven

VIVIANA

when Toya got busted and I rushed out of the train station I was completely freaked out. I was totally paranoid that the cops would come chasing after me as well, which forced me to keep looking over my shoulder. I didn't really feel as if I'd gotten away until I was on the bus heading back home. I rested my head against the window of the bus, closed my eyes and relived everything that went down. I felt bad about cutting out on her, but jail was the last place I wanted or needed to go. I figured Toya knew her way around the judicial system and would find a way out of the mess she was in. By the time I arrived back home I'd completely justified my actions. Because there was no way I was going down for a friend who'd, on that very same day, threatened to do me bodily harm.

When I got home, both my mother and Martin were gone. I was sort of hoping that my mother would be there because I could've really used someone to talk to. There were people I knew from other neighborhoods, but it had been a long time since I'd reached out to them. I suppose if I'd had a computer and an internet connection I could have gone online and talked to some anonymous person, but neither Martin nor my mother felt having a laptop was important.

Sitting in an empty and quiet apartment could drive even the most sane person crazy, so I decided to take another long walk to the beach to kill time and figure out what to do next. I had to come up with a plan for how I was going to convince my mother to break up with Martin and find us a place to live. If I couldn't persuade her, then I had a backup plan of striking out and making it on my own. I figured that I was young, healthy and could do just about anything. I'd have to drop out of high school, of course, but that was pretty much a waste of time anyway. I had never fit in with any of the school cliques. I wasn't popular. I wasn't a cheery-o-cheerleader, and I definitely wasn't the brainy type. The drug kids were cool to a certain extent. I mean, I could smoke weed with seasoned pros, but it wasn't like I went out of my way to do it. The kids at my school and around my neighborhood were into everything from sniffing markers to doing methamphetamines, which made them act crazy as hell. Still, if I wanted to be honest with myself, I did sort of miss hanging out with them at house parties. One of these days I'd go back and make up for lost time.

I figured that if I needed money bad enough, I'd put on some dark sunglasses, pretend I was blind and stand on a street corner selling pencils. But I knew I wouldn't have to go to the extreme. Fast-food places were always looking for help. I could work two part-time jobs and make it. Who knew? If I got lucky, by chance I'd meet a cool guy who was into helping birds like me who had a broken wing.

Finally, I arrived at the beach and just chilled out. I did my usual thing, stuck my toes in the sand and watched people. Then out of nowhere this stranger decided to strike up a conversation with me. I humored him because he looked like the cartoon character from *The Boondocks* comic strip. He tried to get me to give up my phone number, but I just wasn't feeling the guy like that. Besides, he was way too short.

When I got back home, my mother and Martin were still not there. I was hungry, so I checked the refrigerator for something to eat. I was so glad to see a pizza box with several slices still left. I heated up the pizza and then sat down to watch television. I ended up watching a rerun of a program called *Glee*. I really liked the character Sue, who was a mean-spirited gym coach. I identified with her because she just didn't give a damn about anything except her own interests. By the time the show ended, the sun had gone down and the streetlights came on. I was busy channel surfing, trying to find something else of interest to watch, when I heard someone on the sidewalk scream out my name.

"Yo, Viviana!" the voice yelled out. I crept over to the window and peeped downstairs.

"Yo, Viviana, I know you hear me, girl! I know your apartment is somewhere in the building." It was Toya's man, and he was holding his son. I raised up the window and leaned out.

"What do you want?" I asked.

"Yo, girl, where Toya at?" he asked.

"She hasn't called you yet?" I asked.

"Hell, no!" he barked.

"She got jammed up," I explained.

He lowered his head and said, "Damn! Do you know where they took her?"

"No. I didn't stick around for all that."

"Okay, look, you're going to have to hold on to Junior for me. I've got some business to take care of and I can't leave him with his blind great-grandmother." He tried to gain my sympathy, but there was no way I was about to take care of his son.

"I don't know anything about taking care of a baby. You need to take him with you," I said.

He threaded his eyebrows together and spoke more forcefully. "Come on, now. Toya told me y'all was tight. Why can't you just watch him for me while I make this quick run?"

"Toya and I are tight, but not that cool. That's your son. You should take pride in keeping him. My father took me with him everywhere when I was little like your son," I said.

"I'll bet he didn't take you to the bathroom," he snapped.

"That comment was way too ignorant to respond to. Later, man," I said and tucked my head back inside the apartment. Just before I shut the window he saluted me with his middle finger. In kind, I turned my butt toward the window and smacked my fanny. He caught my drift the same way I caught his.

I sat up and watched television hoping to catch my mother when she came home. At five o'clock I finally gave up and went to bed. I had waited up all night on her and she never showed up.

"Viviana," I heard someone whispering my name and shaking my shoulder.

"Leave me alone," I grumbled and turned over in the bed. All I wanted to do was sleep.

"Get up," the voice whispered. I then realized that it was my mother.

"No. Let me sleep. I stayed up all night waiting on you. Now you will just have to wait on me." I closed my eyes tighter, hoping that I'd float back into a deep sleep. My mother yanked the bedspread off me.

"What the hell!" I opened my eyes and glared at her angrily. However, I quickly dropped my evil expression when I saw her bruised face. Her left eye was nearly closed shut, her lip was still bleeding, and the right side of her face was black-and-blue. I didn't have to ask what happened. I already knew that it was Martin. I snatched both the knife and stun gun from beneath my pillow and sprang to my feet.

"Where is he?" I asked, gripping the knife tighter. I was ready to declare war on Martin.

"Viviana, we have to go," she whispered.

"No, he can't get away with this!" I was fired up and angry.

"Viviana, stop fighting me, please. Right now I just need you to come with me," my mother desperately pleaded with me.

"We should at least call an ambulance and the police," I said, wanting to help and make sure that Martin paid the price.

"No. I don't want to deal with the police and I hate hospitals. They'll ask too many questions, get social services involved, and you'll end up in foster care somewhere until they can find housing for us. Just grab what you can and come with me." I unenthusiastically gathered up my belong-

ings and placed them in a large duffel bag while my mother
watched. Once I had everything, I quietly walked out of the
apartment with my mother. When we got outside she put
on sunglasses to hide her wounds. We walked up to Martin
Luther King Jr. Drive, where we hailed a taxi.

"Where are we going?" I asked once I got situated.

"To your grandmother's house," my mother answered.

"But you don't get along with her. Will she even let us
in?" I asked.

"She'll always let us in," my mother whispered. She gave
the cab driver the address, then leaned back and rested her
head against the back of the seat. I looped my arm behind her
neck, cradled her shoulder and pulled her closer to me. I'd
made up my mind that I was going to protect her. I wasn't
going to let anything or anyone hurt her anymore.

When my mother and I arrived at the doorstep of Grandmother Esmeralda's home, I was as shocked as America was
when Barack Obama won the presidency to see my goody-
two-shoes cousin Maya. She looked at my mother and me
as if we were beneath her, and that really pissed me off.
Once we were inside, Grandmother Esmeralda removed my
mother's dark sunglasses and both she and Maya gasped at
her bruised face.

"What happened to you?" Grandmother Esmeralda asked
my mother.

"Nothing," my mother answered. "It's not that bad."

"Have you seen yourself?" Grandmother Esmeralda asked.
"What mean man have you gotten with this time? I swear,

your father must be turning over in his grave. This is not the life he wanted for you."

"Mother, I don't need one of your damn lectures right now!" Salena said.

"Fine, I'll fix you up and ask questions later," Grandmother Esmeralda said.

"Viviana, are you hurt anywhere?" she also asked.

"No. I'm good," I answered.

"Then visit with your cousin Maya while I fix up Salena. You guys haven't seen each other in a long time. You should have plenty to talk about." Grandmother Esmeralda took my mother by the hand and led her down the hallway toward the bathroom.

I looked over at Maya and sized her up. Her shoulder-length black hair looked a little messy, and she had a dumb-ass look on her face and her nose was scrunched up. She looked as if she smelled some foul dog crap. Her skin tone was smooth and even, and her clothes didn't look shabby and outdated like mine. Everything about her demeanor said that she was a perfect princess and was appalled to see that the family peasants had arrived.

"If you don't take that ignorant look off your face I'm going to smack it off!" I said, feeling the need to spit on her feet.

"What look?" she asked innocently.

"Stop pretending as if you don't know what I'm talking about," I said as I walked into the living room where the fireplace was. I walked over to the mantel and looked at all the photographs that Grandmother Esmeralda had placed there. I saw an old school photo of myself when I was in third grade.

"So, where are the other members of your royal family?" I asked, referring to her parents as well as her brother and sister.

"They're not here. I came to visit for a little while."

I looked over my shoulder at Maya.

"Well, isn't that special. You came out of your castle to come and live among the common folk," I said sarcastically.

"Like, what are you talking about? Are you trying to say that I'm like a snob or something?" Maya asked.

"Like a snob or something," I mocked her words. I came across another photo, of Maya and me when we were about eight years old. We were dressed all in white and holding candles. I remembered the photo because my father had taken it. Maya sat down on the sofa positioned against a wall.

"So, what have you been up to lately?" she politely asked.

"You sound like a programmed Barbie doll. Just pull the string and you'll ask the same dumb questions," I spat.

"Look, if you don't want to talk, I totally understand," Maya said, once again sounding like the perfect princess, and it was really aggravating me.

"Shut up, Maya," I commanded.

"Excuse me?" she said, clearly offended.

"Oh, did I hurt your little delicate feelings? You always were a prissy little sap, Maya."

"And you were always a ghetto 'hood rat," she fired back.

I knew I'd gotten beneath her skin.

"And proud of it," I quickly responded. "So, what brings you down from your high tower to visit the common folk?"

"I don't live in a high tower, Viviana," she said. I took a seat in a chair in the opposite corner of the room.

"Yeah, whatever. So, what brings you down here? You and your family rarely visit."

"Well, it doesn't look as if you visit that often either," Maya said.

"Trust me. I visit a heck of a lot more than you do," I said.

"I wanted to spend time with Grandmother Esmeralda," Maya said. But I didn't believe the line of bologna she was trying to feed me.

"Fine, if you don't want to talk about it, I totally understand," I mocked her once again.

"This conversation is going nowhere. You're way too immature," Maya whined as she rose to her feet to leave the room.

"Ha, that's a laugh. If I remember correctly, you're the one who tried to pretend that you were fourteen when you were only eleven because you liked that boy Ray who sang in the church choir."

"Why are you bringing up old stuff? That happened years ago." Maya acted as if she didn't want to remember the time I was talking about.

"Oh, so you don't remember that?" I asked.

"Like I said, that was a long time ago," Maya said unapologetically. "So, what about all of the things I've heard about you?"

"You haven't heard a thing about me," I said, curling the corner of my mouth.

"I heard that you need professional help. It's no secret that after your father died you attempted to kill yourself several times. What was that about?"

I got very angry with her, pointed my finger and squinted

my eyes until they were nearly shut. "Don't you *ever* talk to me about my father!"

"Why? He wasn't nothing but a thug and a gangbanger."

I rose to my feet and got close to her, and dared her to say something else bad about my father.

"What? I'm supposed to be afraid of you now?" Maya asked.

"You need to be because you never know what I might do."

"You'd better back up off me." Maya tried to play like she was a tough girl.

"Our day is going to come. You just better be glad it's not today," I said, stepping away from her.

"What happened to you?" Maya asked.

"The same thing that happened you," I said, sizing her up once again.

"I said that I'm fine and I don't want to go to the hospital!" I heard my mother fussing. I glanced in the direction of the bathroom.

"Are you going to go check on your mother, or are you going to stand here hating on me for no reason?" Maya asked.

"Oh, I have my reasons for not liking you and you know exactly what they are," I said. Maya dropped her eyes toward the floor with guilty shame. "Yeah, I haven't forgotten about what you did." I reminded her of how she should feel at fault. In that instant, if my eyes had been laser beams, Maya would have been incinerated beyond recognition.

"How are you two getting along in here?" Grandmother Esmeralda entered the room. I didn't say anything, but my murderous eyes were shouting. Maya finally broke the silence and tried to downplay the tension between us.

"Everything is fine—we're just catching up."

Grandmother Esmeralda chose to ignore the disquiet between Maya and me. She elected to smile at Maya before turning her attention to me. "Are you okay? Did you see who did that to your mother?"

"No," I answered. "But I have a good idea of who did it."

"Was it the security guard she was dating?" Grandmother Esmeralda asked.

"No, she broke up with him a long time ago. She has a new idiot named Martin who is responsible," I said. "I swear before God, the next time I see him, he's going to have to deal with me," I said in my meanest voice.

"You will do no such thing, Viviana. Nor are you a match for a man. You will only get yourself killed." Grandmother Esmeralda paused in thought. "I just don't understand this thing she has with abusive men. She's too old to have this type of problem."

"People get beat down every day. Weren't you the one who was always saying, 'You're never too old to get your butt beat?'" In some small way I got a twisted pleasure by making her eat her own words.

"Yes, but…" Grandmother Esmeralda stopped talking briefly. "Never mind, it's not worth arguing the point."

"Well, it is what it is," I said, feeling my heart turning into stone.

"Your grandfather was the best father and husband in the world. He never raised a hand to me or his children. He loved us so much. If he were still alive, he'd be so hurt by this. I wish I could make Salena understand that love does not have a fist. I don't understand why she is like that."

"Well, apparently, she missed that lesson," I spoke out sarcastically. Grandmother Esmeralda honed in on my negative attitude.

"Viviana, your mouth is filthy and it is going to get you into big trouble one day if you don't clean it up. Why can't you be more like Maya? She's a good girl. She only makes little teenage mistakes here and there, but overall she's a very respectable young lady. She doesn't have such a bad attitude like you do. You could learn so much from her."

I curled my lips into a sour frown when she suggested I become more like Maya. She was the last person I wanted to emulate.

"Are those your clothes in that bag?" asked Grandmother Esmeralda, pointing to my bag.

"Yeah," I answered, glancing down at my old, dirty duffel bag. For a moment I allowed my thoughts to be seduced with the fantasy of hurling the sack of laundry at Maya's head.

"When was the last time they were washed?" she asked.

I shrugged my shoulders and said, "I don't know, but it's about time for them to be cleaned."

"Fine, take them down to the laundry room. You know where it is. There is plenty of laundry detergent down there," Grandmother Esmeralda said as she exhaled and then collapsed on the sofa. She combed her fingers through her hair and then glanced at the ceiling. Maya sat next to her and hugged her in an effort to comfort her.

"What a suck-up," I mumbled as I picked up my sack of clothes and headed toward the laundry room.

# twelve

*MAYA*

It was well after midnight before Viviana and I got a chance to go to bed. While in the bathroom brushing my teeth I thought about what Viviana used to be like. I didn't like the new version of her. She'd grown into the type of girl who'd beat anyone down in a heartbeat at the slightest hint of disrespect.

Viviana and I grew up together and spent the summer months at our grandmother's home. We went to church together, played with our dolls together, combed each other's hair, and danced to our favorite music in Grandmother Esmeralda's backyard. We were inseparable back then. Grandmother Esmeralda loved to take us everywhere with her. We'd do fun things like hang out at the beach, go shopping, and at one point Viviana and I were both taking ballet lessons. When Viviana and I were nine years old, Grandmother Esmeralda took us to Disney World. We had so much fun that summer. By the time we'd turned twelve, Viviana had discovered that she liked boys. They were just okay to me, but it wasn't like I was truly interested in them at that age. However, Viviana convinced me that having a boyfriend would make us look mature. So that summer we started getting into a little mischief with the twin brothers Revell and Reggie, who used to live next door to Grandmother Esmeralda. They both had high-pitched voices, laughed obnoxiously and had bad acne. Neither one was particularly cute, but for Viviana and me, we were only having a little fun. That was until we ended up experiencing our first kiss together.

One hot afternoon, Grandmother Esmeralda left the house to run a quick errand. Viviana and I were hanging out in the backyard drinking Kool-Aid and thumbing through fashion magazines. Viviana decided to call Reggie so that he and his brother could come over and take advantage of the time that our grandmother was away. Both Revell and Reggie came out of the house immediately and jumped the fence that separated our yards. I'll be the first to admit that I was having fun being chased around and screaming at the top of my voice. I didn't want Revell to catch me, but then again I did. They cornered us on opposite sides of the same tree. Without asking, Revell pressed his lips against mine and I angrily pushed him off me. Reggie was doing the same to Viviana, but she liked it. Their lips were smashed together and they just kept turning their heads back and forth. I, of course, thought it was gross because at the time it just seemed like they were sharing each other's spit. Revell begged me to get with the program and be more like Viviana, but I was a good girl and just didn't do stuff like that. Viviana thought I was so lame. Revell, who wasn't about to be outdone by his brother, pressed up against me and tried to steal a kiss. I once again fought him off and told Viviana that I didn't think it was such a good idea to call them up and invite them over.

Viviana broke away from her kissing session and said, "Stop being so afraid, Maya. It's a lot of fun if you'd just relax."

"Yeah. Just relax and let me do the work." Revell tried to use a low and commanding voice, but it only cracked and released an irritating pitch right in the middle of his sentence.

"I don't think so," I said, wanting both boys to leave before Grandmother Esmeralda returned.

"Revell, you should leave," I said, pointing in the direction of his house.

"No. Just let me get to second base. Look at Viviana and my brother. She's letting him go to second base." Revell once again begged me to let my guard down. I held my ground and firmly told him no. I walked back to the house, entered it and stood behind the safety of the screen door. Then, just as I'd feared, Grandmother Esmeralda returned home and caught Viviana kissing and getting felt up.

I closed my eyes for a second and erased the memory from my thoughts. I tied up my hair and headed toward the bedroom. When I entered, Viviana was just pulling back the bedcovers.

"You can use the washroom now," I said politely.

"What for?" Viviana asked.

"To wash your face and brush your teeth. There is a spare toothbrush in the medicine cabinet," I said.

"I don't see the purpose of brushing my teeth before I go to bed when I'm just going to wake up with morning breath anyway," she said.

"It's part of having good hygiene," I explained.

Viviana met my gaze. "So, what are you saying? That I stink or something?"

I knew right away that she'd gotten offended. "That's not what I said."

"But that's what you're implying, right?" Viviana stepped close to me and I backed away.

"I wasn't trying to be insulting. You've taken my comment way too seriously," I said.

Viviana glared at me with heat in her eyes. The old Viviana that I used to get along with was long gone. "Why don't you just leave me alone and go get in your own bed?" she said.

"Uhm, don't you remember what our grandmother said? We have to share the bed."

"I'm not sharing this bed. I was here first, so it's mine." Viviana got in the bed and pulled the covers up to her shoulder.

"So where am I supposed to sleep?" I asked.

"On the floor, *princess*," Viviana said.

"Oh, no! There is no *way* that I'm sleeping on the floor." That was where I drew the line.

"You want to fight for the bed?" Viviana asked. She tossed back the covers and rose to her feet.

"Come on, take your best shot," she encouraged me to bring it.

"What's the matter with you? Why can't you just let what happened in the past go?" I asked, trying to reason with her.

"It's not that easy, *princess*," she said, waiting for me to make my first move.

"This is stupid and ghetto," I said, turning my back to her.

I walked over to a nearby closet and pulled out a blanket and another pillow. I glanced at Viviana with disgust and exited the bedroom. I went downstairs, figuring that I'd sleep on the sofa. However, when I got there, Salena was already asleep on it. I grumbled quietly to myself and walked back upstairs. I entered Grandmother Esmeralda's bedroom. She was already in a deep sleep, so I crawled into bed with her, curled my body up and closed my eyes.

When I awoke the following morning Grandmother Esmeralda wasn't beside me. Her bed was so comfortable that I toyed with the idea of never leaving it. I turned onto my side and snuggled up with one of the pillows to try and get more sleep. Just as I was about to close my eyes, something told me to turn over. When I did, Viviana was standing over me.

"Aww, the poor princess was too high-strung to sleep on the floor." Viviana didn't waste any time handing out critical remarks.

"Why don't you just go away? I'm not bothering you," I grumbled as I turned back over.

"Trust me. I wish I could go someplace far away and just be by myself." Viviana's voice had a sad undertone to it, so I turned back over to face her. I thought that perhaps she was in a slightly better mood.

"Where would you go?" I asked.

"I don't know. Just someplace where life is easy."

"Do you like reading books at all?"

"What does reading some stupid book have to do with anything?" she asked mockingly.

"Well. For a lot of people reading a book can be sort of like escaping from your own reality. It's worked for me a few times. I thought maybe it'd work for you, too."

Viviana laughed. "That's the dumbest thing I've ever heard of. But I'm not surprised, especially since it came from your mouth."

"Whatever, Viviana. I was only trying to help."

"What I need help with is getting money to get my own place. Me and my friend Toya talked about living together," Viviana said as she sat down in a chair in the corner of the room.

"You're too young to live on your own." I thought to myself that her idea was truly a dumb one.

"No, I'm not. I know what life is really about. I've been places, seen and done things. I'm not some sheltered princess who lives in la-la land like you." Viviana didn't let up for even a second with her personal attacks on me.

"Just for your information, my life isn't as perfect as you think it is," I said, feeling the need to defend myself.

"Yeah, right. You practically have a silver spoon in your mouth. I'll even bet you that Aunt Raven and your father, Herman, have even set up a college fund for you." Viviana had a contemptuous frown on her face.

"Well, yeah. Of course they do," I said. To me, saving for college was just as normal as back-to-school shopping.

"You guys still living in that big house out in the suburbs?" Viviana asked.

"Our house is small," I said, feeling the need to make her feel better.

"When I do get settled down, the place that I'm going to

live in is going to be twenty times bigger than yours. I'm going to have everything in it. Maids, cooks, a ton of clothes and lots of jewelry. You just wait. I'll show you."

"How do you plan on getting all of that stuff?" I asked.

"I'm going to steal it. Well, most of it, anyway," she said without batting an eye.

"Are you serious?" I asked.

"Yup. Like I said, my girlfriend Toya hooked me up and taught me how to pick pockets and stuff. She can make more money in one day than your dad probably makes in a week," Viviana boasted.

"But what if you get caught?" I asked.

"I'm too smart to get caught," Viviana said stubbornly.

"Don't tell me you're dumb enough to think you'd never get caught. Now you're starting to sound like your father." I shook my head disapprovingly. Before I could react she had wedged her forearm between my neck and shoulder and pressed down. I struggled as I placed my hand on her elbow and tried to push her off me.

"If you ever make fun of my father again, I swear to God I will choke you in your sleep! You of all people should know that!" Viviana pressed down harder, which caused me to cough.

I gasped for air and said, "You're choking me." Viviana pressed down hard one more time before she lifted her weight off me. As I tried to calm my labored breathing, she chuckled and said, "Now you know exactly how much I don't like you."

Viviana hovered over me and observed as I caught my breath and curled up into the fetal position. Once I caught my breath, the only thing on my mind was retribution for what she'd just done. There was no way that I was going to let her little stunt go unanswered. I scooted over to the other side of the bed and got out of it. I moved around the bed toward Viviana with one thought in mind. *Pull all of her freaking hair off her head.* Viviana smirked. She knew that what she'd done would cause a fight and she welcomed the confrontation. Just as I about to make my move on her, I heard Grandmother Esmeralda shouting at Salena. I stopped cold in my tracks and listened.

"Why won't you get help?" I heard Grandmother Esmeralda ask.

"Because I don't need any, Mother!" Salena shouted back. I heard the sound of glass shattering and rushed out of the room. I hustled down the stairs and ran back toward the kitchen. Grandmother Esmeralda had grabbed a broom from the corner of the room and began to sweep up the broken glass from an empty wine bottle. I glanced over at my aunt Salena, who'd just popped open a second bottle of wine that Grandmother Esmeralda had. Salena put the bottle up to her swollen lips, tossed her head back and guzzled down the liquor like water running down a drain.

"Is everything okay?" I asked nervously, concerned for both of them. Aunt Salena smeared away the excess liquor with the back of her hand. She looked a little better, but not much. She had a nasty-looking black eye and puffy lips.

"What are you staring at?" She belched, clearly annoyed with the way I was staring at her.

"Salena, think about Viviana. Think of what this is doing to her. It's not a good thing to raise a child in an abusive home." Grandmother Esmeralda tried to speak as lovingly and as calmly as she could. "You need help. This man you're with is no good for you. We could go to church and talk to the priest and—"

Salena interrupted. "So, what are you saying? That I'm not a good mother? That I'm not as good as Raven? Viviana isn't as good or as smart as Maya?" Aunt Salena had completely snapped. I'd never seen the bitter and angry side of her.

"I did not say that." Grandmother Esmeralda was again trying to remain calm in an explosive situation.

"I'll finish cleaning that up," I said as I moved toward my grandmother and took the broom from her.

"You've always liked Raven better than me. Everything Raven did was always perfect to you and Papa. Nothing I ever did was good enough. I struggled to get good grades and Raven was an A student. Raven went to college, and I dropped out to work so that I could help out financially when Papa started getting sick and couldn't work anymore. But did I get so much as a thank-you or any type of appreciation? No. You said it was my duty to help out while Raven was away having the time of her life in college. I helped to pay for her college education." Salena took another long gulp of the liquor.

"Salena. I told you that you didn't have to drop out of college. I told you that I was taking a second job," said Grandmother Esmeralda.

"No, Mama. You're twisting it around so that you don't look bad. You told me that Raven was the smart one. You said that Raven would finish and make you and Papa proud."

"Salena, you're talking crazy. You're forty years old talking about things that happened twenty years ago. You can't change the past."

"And you can't forget it either, Mama."

"I worry about you, Salena. Why won't you let me help you? You can stay here, away from that mean man who beats you."

"No, Mama. That man loves me. I know he does, and we are going to be happy together. You'll see," Salena said, taking yet another gulp of wine.

"Give me the wine. You've had enough."

"No!" Salena held the alcohol close to her.

"Love is not violent, Salena. If he beats you he doesn't love or care about you," Grandmother Esmeralda said.

A slow yet hideous smiled spread across Salena's face. "Our love is special, Mama. And it's stronger than the love you and Papa had. It's a hundred times stronger and nothing and no one is going to take him away from me." Aunt Salena pivoted and walked toward the front door.

"Where are you going?" Grandmother Esmeralda followed her.

"Back to Martin," Salena said as she opened the door.

"Why are you so difficult!" Grandmother Esmeralda shouted.

"Because you made me that way, Mama." Salena stumbled out into the morning sunlight.

"What about Viviana?" asked my grandmother as I walked up behind her. Aunt Salena didn't answer as she staggered down the sidewalk. Grandmother Esmeralda exhaled loudly as she stepped back inside.

"Do you want some breakfast?" she asked as she headed toward the kitchen.

"I'll make you some breakfast this time," I said. Grandmother Esmeralda stood still for a moment and placed her hands into prayer position. She prayed silently for a moment before going into the kitchen. I glanced up and noticed Viviana standing at the top of the staircase. Our eyes met for a brief moment before she turned her back and entered the bathroom behind her.

The following day Grandmother Esmeralda drove me back home. She wanted to talk to my mother face-to-face about all the drama that had gone down. I was excited because I'd get to go back home and hang out at the pool with Keysha and see Misalo once again. Although I wasn't gone for very long, I felt as if I'd been away for an eternity. The only thing that I didn't like about going back home was that Viviana had to come with us. When we pulled into my driveway my mother came out. Once I got out of the car she gave me a quick hug and then waited for Viviana to exit.

"Oh, my goodness, Viviana, look at you. You've grown so much," my mother said gleefully as she hugged her. Viviana reluctantly hugged her back as she took in her surroundings.

"Hello, Mama," my mother greeted Grandmother Esmeralda. They embraced each other before heading back inside. I noticed that my grandmother was limping.

"What's wrong?" I asked.

"I'm getting old and I'm falling apart," she said as she entered the house. Once inside, my little brother and sister rushed over to her for their hug. I immediately went upstairs to my room to check things out. I wanted to make sure that Anna hadn't been in there bothering my things. The first place I checked was my closet for any missing clothes.

"So, this is your princess chamber." Viviana walked into my room uninvited.

"What are you doing up here?" I asked, wanting her to leave.

"Just checking it out. Your old house was much smaller than this one. Obviously, you guys are wealthy," she said. Viviana opened up one of the drawers of my jewelry box, which was situated in a corner.

"Get out of there!" I said and moved over to where she stood. I closed the drawer and waited for her to back out of my room.

"Oh, it's like that?" Viviana had the nerve to be surprised by my attitude toward her.

"It's like that and a whole lot more." I didn't restrain my words or disdain for her.

Viviana smirked and then chuckled. "You don't have a damn thing in here that I want anyway." She started to back out of my room.

"Oh, there you are." My little sister had just come upstairs. "How are you? It's so good to see you again," Anna said as she gave Viviana a hug.

"It's good to see you, too, Anna," Viviana said. For some reason the two of them were very fond of each other. They always had been. I shut my door so that I could have some privacy.

About an hour later, I was dressed and ready to go hang out at the pool. I'd already phoned both Keysha and Misalo and told them to meet me there. When I walked into the kitchen my mother and grandmother were sitting at the kitchen table talking.

"I'm going to go to the pool for a while," I informed my mother.

"Okay. Viviana and Anna headed over there about fifteen minutes ago," said my mother. I rolled my eyes as I walked out the door.

When I arrived at the pool, I saw Keysha with dark sunglasses on, sitting in a chair, sipping on a strawberry smoothie. I walked over and sat beside her.

"See, that's not even right, girl. Where did you get that smoothie? It looks so good," I said, wishing that I had one.

"I made it," Keysha said with a smile.

"Let me taste it," I said, extending my hand.

"I brought two. You can have the other one. It's in the freezer inside the clubhouse," she said.

"Oh, you're the best," I said as I went to retrieve the drink.

When I returned I got comfortable and said, "You would not believe all of the drama that went down at my grandmother's house."

"I was wondering why you hadn't called me," Keysha said.

"Girl, all kinds of crazy stuff happened," I said. "My aunt got beat up by her boyfriend, and my nutty cousin Viviana hates my guts."

"What?" Keysha blurted out loudly.

"Shh. You don't have to let the entire pool know," I said.

"I'm sorry. Come on, spill it. Tell me how everything went down." I told her every detail of my visit with my grandmother. She sat and listened, but interrupted me when I mentioned Viviana's friend Toya.

"Wait a minute. Hold the hell up." Keysha stopped me. "Where was Viviana living that she knows a girl named Toya who steals?" she asked.

"I don't know," I said. Keysha leaned back in her seat and lifted her glasses off her face. "Why?" I asked.

"I'm just wondering if Viviana's Toya and the Toya I used to hang out with are one and the same person."

"Who is this Toya chick? You've never mentioned her before," I asked.

"We used to hang together a long time ago. Toya and I would go around shoplifting," Keysha explained.

"OMG, you used to go shoplifting? Why?" I asked, totally stunned by this news.

"Times were hard," Keysha said. "I was a different person back then. That was before I knew who my father was and long before I moved out here to live with him. Now I've just got to know if it's the same Toya."

"Well, Viviana and my bratty sister are supposed to be here," I said, searching around the pool deck for them.

"Wait a minute." Keysha tapped my thigh. "They're just now walking in. Oh, she does look rough, Maya."

"I told you. That chick is *loca,*" I said.

"Call her over here," Keysha said.

"Do I have to?" I complained.

"Yes. I've just got to know if she and I know the same Toya," Keysha said anxiously.

"Anna!" I called to my sister to get her attention and then

waved her over. She and Viviana walked over to where Keysha and I were sitting.

"What do you want?" Anna asked.

"I wanted to introduce Viviana to Keysha," I said.

"Hello," Keysha greeted Viviana.

"Hey," Viviana replied.

"Viviana, Keysha has a question for you," I said.

"What kind of question?" Viviana asked suspiciously.

"It's not that kind of question," Keysha interjected. "I was just wondering where in Chicago do you live?"

"Why? Do you want to make fun of me or something?" Viviana put her hands on her hips.

"No, it's nothing like that," Keysha said. "I'm just trying to figure out if we know the same person."

"I doubt it," Viviana said.

"Well, you just never know. I didn't always live out here," Keysha explained.

"You seem like you've lived out here in the lap of luxury all your life." Viviana didn't filter her words or attitude.

"You live off of King Drive, don't you?" Keysha asked.

"And what if I do?" Viviana asked.

"Toya Taylor," Keysha blurted out. When Keysha said the name, Viviana's eyes lit up.

"You know her?" Viviana asked.

"Yeah, we used to hang out back in the day." At that moment Viviana popped her fingers.

"So, you're the Keysha that she was telling me about. She hates your guts," Viviana informed her.

"Well, the feeling is mutual," Keysha fired back. "I used to live in the same building as her."

"Well, that makes two of us. It's a small world," Viviana said.

"Well, great. Are we done here?" Anna asked. "I want to show her around."

"Oh, sure," I said, glancing over at Keysha. "We just wanted to know if you guys knew the same person."

"I take it that you've told Cleopatra here about everything that's gone down between us," Viviana said.

"Now, hold up. My name isn't Cleopatra," Keysha snapped at Viviana.

"Whatever, chick," Viviana said as Anna pulled her away from us.

"That girl has a serious attitude," Keysha said.

"I told you. I can't wait for her to leave," I said.

"Well, let me say this to you. If she's friends with Toya Taylor, your cousin is bad news. Trust me, I know. My crazy brother, Mike, tried to date Toya and she really played him."

"What was Mike doing trying to date a girl like Toya?" I asked.

"He was thinking with the little head, if you catch my drift." Both Keysha and I cracked up laughing. While we were in the middle of laughing, Cocky Carlo, the new guy with the shifty eyes, walked up.

"Hey, ladies," he greeted us with his bright smile and cute dimples.

"Hello," Keysha and I responded simultaneously.

"Mind if I pull up a chair and join you?" Before I could say, "Go away," he'd sat himself down next to me. Keysha and I looked at each other and then back at him.

"Am I interrupting something?" Carlo asked.

"Don't you think you're being just a little bit bold?" Keysha asked.

"Probably," he answered and then smiled charmingly.

"What Keysha is trying to say is that we're having a private conversation," I explained.

"And I'm intruding, right?" Carlo nodded his head knowingly.

"Are you always this quick, honey?" Keysha asked.

"Okay. I can see that I'm not really welcome right now, but I wanted to stop and meet you." He focused his attention on me.

"Can I ask what your name is?"

I looked deeply into Carlo's eyes and momentarily got lost in them.

"Maya," I said slowly and softly.

"Well, Maya, I'm Carlo. I'm kind of new around here," he said and reached for my hand. He held it and said, "I haven't seen you around lately, but I'm glad I ran into you today. I'd like to take you out sometime." I don't know why I didn't say that I had a boyfriend. I think I was in shock. "Just think about it. We can go anywhere you want to. I have my own car."

"Really? You have your own car?" I sounded like I'd been temporarily drugged. I was caught in his net.

"Yeah," he answered. He took a pen from his pocket and turned my hand to expose my palm. He wrote his phone number in the middle of my hand. "Seriously, call me sometime," he said and then turned my hand over and kissed the back of it. I was absolutely transfixed; lost in his eyes.

"What's going on?" Misalo had finally arrived and I snapped out of it.

"Nothing," I quickly answered him. Cocky Carlo rose to his feet and sized up Misalo. He was taller than Misalo and much more muscular.

"Adios, Maya. It was nice meeting you," Cocky Carlo said before he stepped away.

"What was that about, Maya?" Misalo asked, distrustfully.

"Nothing, baby, he was just some guy," I said, closing my palm to hide Carlo's phone number.

"It looked like more than that to me. I saw the way he was looking at you, and how he kissed your hand. Are you cheating on me or something?" Misalo was clearly more upset than I realized.

"Woo, I think it's time for me to go for a swim," Keysha said, excusing herself.

"Look at you. Getting all jealous over nothing," I said as I stood and stepped into his embrace. We kissed passionately. When I opened my eyes, I glanced over his shoulders and met Viviana's gaze. She looked totally envious of me. I stuck my tongue out at her as I caressed the back of Misalo's head.

# thirteen

*VIVIANA*

Grandmother Esmeralda and I arrived home before sunset. She hated driving at night because she couldn't see as well. I was thankful that we stopped and got take-out Chinese food for dinner, beef fried rice, egg foo young and shrimp egg rolls. The food smelled so good and I just couldn't wait to dig in. As soon as we entered the house, I pulled off my sneakers, left them at the door, and followed her into the kitchen. She set the food on top of the stove before heading to the bathroom. I grabbed a plate and fork from the cupboard, ripped open the brown bag, pulled out the white containers and opened the lids. I was starving.

"Go wash your hands first," said Grandmother Esmeralda, who was returning from the bathroom.

"Nah, I don't need to," I said. I was about to pull out one of the crispy egg rolls and take a bite. Before I knew anything, she was standing next to me slapping the back of my hand. Instinctively, I knuckled up my fists and prepared to defend myself.

"Go do what I told you. Your hands are filthy. Look at all

of the black dirt under your fingernails." I unclenched my fists and took a peek. She was right, my hands were dirty.

"Women should always be clean," she said, moving toward the refrigerator and taking out a two-liter bottle of soda. I went into the bathroom and freshened up. When I returned she'd made my plate for me and set it on the table.

"Have a seat. We'll eat dinner together," she said, inviting me to sit down next to her. All I really wanted to do was take my plate of food, go upstairs, sit on the bed and eat. I didn't want to have dinner with her because I knew she'd talk about my mother. I knew there was no way I'd get out of sitting with her, so I decided to suffer through it.

Once I got comfortable in my seat, I reached for my fork and was about to start shoveling food in my mouth.

"Ahem." Grandmother Esmeralda cleared her throat before reaching her hand toward mine.

"Oh, right. We have to say grace." I held on to her hand, bowed my head and listened to her say the blessing.

"Finally," I mumbled as I began eating.

"Have you heard from your mother?" asked Grandmother Esmeralda.

"No," I said, thinking nothing of it.

"Salena never stays in one place for too long. Whenever I get a phone number and address for her it's only good for a few months. I've gotten tired of trying to keep up with you and her," Grandmother Esmeralda said as she ate a small portion of her food.

"We've lived in so many different places I get confused sometimes, too," I said jokingly.

"You shouldn't have to live like that. It's not good for you."

"She'll get it together. I know she will. I'm going to help her by saving up enough money to get us an apartment," I said, defending my mother while attempting to prove that all hope wasn't lost.

"Salena believes that she can't survive without a man in her life. She is so jealous of Raven and wants everything she has. Salena doesn't know how to be herself. She always changes in order to make her man happy, and that's not the way love goes." Grandmother Esmeralda paused in thought and then said, "Her mind is stuck in the past and she is still trying to compete with her older sister. I don't know what can be done to fix this."

"After my father passed away she was never the same," I said.

"Your father was no good for her." I stopped eating and glared at my grandmother.

"God bless him, but he and his entire family were cursed," Grandmother Esmeralda said with unwavering conviction.

"What do you mean he was cursed?" I asked.

"Oh, Viviana, don't you remember any of the lessons you learned in church?" she asked. To be honest, I found church boring. Most of the time I either fell asleep or daydreamed while the priest spoke.

"No, I don't," I answered as I bit into my egg roll.

"Sometimes a bad demon can—"

I interrupted her. "Don't tell me you believe in superstition." Grandmother Esmeralda got quiet for a long moment. I could tell there was something very heavy on her heart and mind.

"You're too young and unknowledgeable to understand

the things I am speaking of." Then just as if she'd flipped on a light switch in another room, she dropped that conversation and changed the subject.

"Where do you guys live now?" she asked.

"On the Southside, off of King Drive," I said as I scraped my plate and pushed food onto my fork with my thumb.

"Does she have a phone there?" Grandmother Esmeralda asked.

"Why? Do you want to call her?" I asked. "I have her cell phone number."

"Yes, maybe she's sober now and can talk rationally." Grandmother Esmeralda excused herself and retrieved her cordless phone.

"What's her phone number?" she asked. I told her the numbers to dial. When she did she said, "That cellular number is no longer in service. Are you sure that's the phone number?" she asked.

"I'm positive," I answered. "She probably just forgot to pay the bill."

"See, this is why I can't help her or keep up with her." Grandmother Esmeralda released a frustrated sigh. "Tomorrow we'll go visit her and I'll try to talk some sense into her."

I thought to myself, *Good luck with that one.* The one thing I knew about my mother was that when she was in love, nothing else mattered. Not even me.

After dinner I wanted to go hang out in the streets around her neighborhood. I was hoping to see some old friends that I grew up with. But Grandmother Esmeralda put the brakes on that idea.

"Let's watch a movie together," she said.

"What do you want me to do? Rent a film?" I asked.

"No. Of course not. I have the perfect movie for us to watch. Come follow me," she said. We walked into another room where she had television, a VCR and a few movies.

"Wow, you still have a VCR," I said teasingly.

"We can watch *My Family,*" she said, holding up the video box with a prideful smile. I remembered watching the movie with her as a little girl at least a thousand times. It was as if all of the answers to her dilemmas were contained in that film. She and my mother, Salena, were alike in that regard. When it came to certain things, their minds were trapped in the past.

"What else do you have?" I quickly asked, because I didn't want to suffer through another viewing of that movie.

"I have *Forrest Gump,*" she said.

"Oh, God no, Grandma," I said, searching for something better. To my surprise she had a Tyler Perry movie. Of course, it was about a family.

"Let's watch this one. *Like Water for Chocolate.*" I held up the box.

"Oh, that's a good one. I have not watched that in some time," she said.

"What is it about?" I asked reluctantly, fearing it would be boring.

"Oh, Viviana. It is a movie about family. A family with a very mean mother," Grandmother Esmeralda said. I was about to put it back to see what else she had.

"No, no, no. I want to see it now. There's lots of good cooking in that movie, plus there is a love story that will warm your heart." She chuckled. "There is even a subplot that deals with a family curse that lasted four generations. You'll like it. It has lots of drama."

I popped in the videotape, and sat down next to my grandmother. The movie was in Spanish and I had to sit there and read the subtitles because I didn't understand everything that was being said, only some of it. I just knew that I'd fall asleep watching it. That is, until I saw the cute lover. Just like Grandmother Esmeralda said, the movie was very interesting. It was about three sisters living in Mexico in the early 1900s. The youngest girl, Tita, was not to break tradition and was supposed to take care of her mother until she died. Tita was to never marry, have a husband or children. Then one day a man told her that he loved her and wanted to marry her, but Tita's mother wouldn't allow it. Instead she allowed the lover man to marry Tita's sister. The only reason the lover man agreed to that arrangement was so that he could be near Tita all of the time. There were so many things that the character Tita and I had in common. Both of our mothers were certifiably crazy. We were trapped in a dilemma that we had no control over. Our fathers had passed away, and finally, finding romance for both of us was very difficult.

When the movie concluded, I felt a wave of sadness overcome me, while Grandmother Esmeralda quietly snored next to me. She was right; the movie was very good and touching. I sat there for a moment wishing I had the power and bravery of Tita. I also wanted to learn how to cook like her. She had the ability to place all of her feelings into her food so that, the moment anyone tasted it, they could experience every emotion that she felt when she prepared it. If I could master that trick, I'd be one badass Latina.

I wasn't sleepy and still wanted to go outside, but didn't feel like waking up my grandmother to ask for permission. I was practically an adult and felt as if I could come and go as I pleased. I knew my grandmother slept to the sound of the television, something I'd learned a long time ago, so I flipped the channel to a news station so the noise of the television set remained constant.

I stepped out onto the front porch and into the breezy night air. I looked down the street in one direction and noticed some guy washing his car, which I thought was strange for this time of night. There were also three little kids, who I assumed were his, sprinting around, chasing each other and squealing. I looked in the other direction and saw another guy leaning up against his car door with his girlfriend. She had her rear end pressed against him and had surrendered her neck to his lips.

"It would be so nice to have a boyfriend." I sighed as I sat down in Grandmother Esmeralda's chair. Watching the lovebirds made me think about what had happened earlier when I was with my little cousin Anna.

Anna and I were always cool with each other. Although she was younger than Maya and me by two years, she was fun to hang around because of her outgoing personality. Anna didn't judge people by their clothes or the way they looked. If you were nice to her, she'd be nice to you. It was just that simple with her. Anna immediately got me out of the house, so we could gossip and catch up on how things had been going in our lives.

"I'm so happy you're here. The moment Grandmother Es-meralda told me you were coming I got so excited," Anna said as we walked down the driveway and away from the house. Anna had told her mother that she was taking me to the pool to hang out.

"It's good to see you, too. It has been a long time," I said.

"It's been entirely too long, Viviana," Anna said as we continued down a neighborhood street.

"So, what have you been up to?" I asked.

"Well, when I'm not fighting with Maya, I try to get boys to notice me," she answered.

"Are you kidding? As pretty as you are, you should have boys following you around."

"Ha, I wish. I think I'm cursed. I'm practically invisible to boys. I tried to get Maya to hook me up, but all she did was make me feel bad for wanting to date. Then she got on her soapbox and tried to lecture me as if she were Papa. She's always bossing me and Paul around like that and it's gotten old."

"Really? Maya tries to act like she's your mother?"

"Yeah, she says that she's trying to protect me. And I'm like, I didn't ask for protection services. I just want to party, have a good time and meet boys." Anna laughed and did a quick dance move.

"Look at you," I said, smiling. "You've grown up so much since that summer night we snuck out of Grandmother Es-meralda's house to the hip-hop concert in the park."

"Oh, my God, that was like the best time of my entire life. I'm so serious, Viviana. I'll never forget the time we had. I remember everything about that night."

"Really?" I smiled, recalling the fun we had. "You were only twelve then, right?"

"Yes, but you treated me like I was the same age as you were. I was in seventh grade and you were a freshman in high school. And the guy you were dating, oh, my God, he was so hot! I even remembered that his name was Andy. He was eighteen and a senior in high school. He even drove a Mustang convertible. I remember being so envious of you."

I smiled and then laughed. Anna had a way of making me feel at ease. I didn't feel all defensive around her. "Yeah, Andy was sweet," I admitted.

"Whatever happened to him? I thought for sure you guys would have eloped by now," Anna said.

"Ha, that's a laugh. I had my fun with Andy and then I moved on," I said.

"You moved on? Are you serious?" Anna couldn't believe what I was telling her.

"Yes," I said as I continued to laugh.

"How did you get over the breakup?" Anna asked.

"Well, honey, if there is one thing my mother has taught me it's how to run through men. The best way to get over one guy is to get under another one," I repeated something I'd heard Salena say once.

"So, how many boyfriends have you had since Andy?" Anna asked.

"Too many to count," I spoke truthfully. "I'm just on a dry spell right now. Once things settle down again, I'll get back in the game."

Anna stopped, took my hands into her own and forced me to meet her eyes. "Okay, I know this may sound extreme, but could you please teach me everything you know about boys, dating and whatever. I know that you've experienced things, and I just want to learn from you." Anna looked at me as if my next words would either crush her heart or brighten up her life. I smiled at her. She was like the perfect little sister.

"I'd be happy to," I said.

"Yes!" Anna whispered. "I am so ready for this."

"You're probably just maturing at a faster rate than other kids are," I said.

"See, why is it that you can understand that but no one else can? Do you realize that I had my very first beer with you that night we snuck out of the house?"

"Yeah, I remember that. I thought for sure you were going to tell and get us both in trouble."

"Just like I told you back then—I'm loyal and trustworthy. It was our secret, and it was and still has remained just between us."

"Have you tried to drink anything else since?" I asked.

"No, but I'm willing to try something," Anna said eagerly.

"Okay. I'll keep that in mind."

"I can't believe how much cooler you are than Maya. Had I said something like that to her she would've hit the rooftop. Sometimes I can't stand her and her perfect little relationship with Misalo."

"Misalo? Who is he?" I asked.

"Maya's boyfriend, who she has wrapped around her little finger," Anna stated.

"He's okay, but he is nothing like Carlo." Anna said the boy's name as if he were a god.

"Who is Carlo?" I asked.

"He is the new boy that has moved into the neighborhood and he is so hot. I swear, he can walk on water, Viviana," Anna exaggerated, as we came to a corner and had to wait for the stoplight.

"Is Carlo your boyfriend?" I asked.

"I wish. He doesn't even know that I'm alive. I'd give anything just to be with him. Viviana, I swear, Carlo looks just like Enrique Iglesias. He has thick eyebrows, and long eyelashes and a little stubble on his chin. Every time I see Carlo he takes my breath away."

"Oh, I can't wait to see this guy," I said as we walked into the swimming pool clubhouse. When we arrived Maya was already there.

"How did she get here before us?" I asked.

"She probably took the shortcut," Anna said. "Come on. Let's go sit on the other side of the pool, because I don't want to be anywhere near Maya."

"Yeah, neither do I." As I followed Anna, Maya called to her and waved for us to stop over.

"Damn, what does she want?" Anna griped.

"Who knows," I said as I reluctantly went over by Maya.

By the time Anna and I found a spot to sit away from Maya and Keysha, my dislike for both of them had swelled like a river about to overrun its banks. I didn't like the way Keysha stared at me judgmentally. I could tell Keysha thought she was better than me. Maya didn't make me feel any better, because all she did was look at me with her tiny little nose crinkled up, as if there was some foul odor wafting through the air. Just by looking into their eyes I could tell they both felt as if I were beneath them. I couldn't believe that Keysha would try to pretend as if she knew Toya Taylor. She looked just like Maya, the type of girl who lives a very comfortable life. I knew that Anna was from the same background, but like I said, she was different; she wasn't stuck-up. Anna told me all about how tight Keysha and Maya were.

"They've been best friends for a while now," Anna explained as we lounged on lawn chairs. We observed and gossiped about both of them like they were cheap prostitutes attempting to act as if they came from royalty.

"They do everything together. They've practically created their own little clique. Keysha is like a total slut. She's dated a boy who had an alcohol problem and a sexually transmitted disease. Then she turned around and took some other girl's guy, and come to find out the other girl was pregnant with the guy's baby."

"Oh, that's just wrong," I said as I slid off my shoes. My toes looked like a disaster, and I thought for sure Anna would call me on it, but she didn't and I liked her even more.

"Then Keysha started dating this other guy...."

"I'm tired of hearing about Keysha. Tell me more about Maya and her boyfriend."

"Oh. She is like so head over heels in love with this boy named Misalo. Oh, they make me sick with how they're always all over each other. And they never fight about anything," Anna said.

"What does he look like?" I asked.

"He's okay-looking. Short hair, round face, kind of skinny, though."

"That doesn't sound like the guy who's over there holding her hand." I directed Anna's attention back to Keysha and Maya. Anna expelled a gasp of air as if someone had just punched her in the gut. At that moment I knew the drop-dead gorgeous guy kissing Maya's hand was none other than Carlo.

"Oh, my God! I think I'm going to be sick." Anna turned her back so that she wouldn't see. "Please tell me that he didn't just kiss Maya's hand."

"I'd be lying if I said that."

"Damn. She already has Misalo. Why is Maya going after him?" Anna raised her voice. "She shouldn't even be flirting with him. I swear, I hate her."

"Uhm, you may want to turn back around. I think Misalo just arrived," I informed her.

"What?" Anna spun quickly around.

"You're right. Misalo is kind of scrawny compared to Carlo. And it looks like little Misalo is not too happy with Maya," I said, thinking it would make Anna feel better.

Anna was too lovesick. She wanted Carlo to notice her, and the fact that he had any type of interest in Maya was like a double slap on the cheek. "Do you want me to help you get him?" I asked.

"It's no use." Anna had already given up hope.

"Come on," I said as I slipped my feet back inside my shoes. I stood and grabbed Anna's hand.

"Where are we going?" she asked.

"I'm going to get Carlo to notice you," I said as I hur-riedly made my way across the pool deck. Just as Anna and I were about to walk out I glanced over at Maya, who stuck her tongue out at me. I wanted to run over there and punch her in the face, but I had better things to do.

Once we exited the clubhouse, we found Carlo leaning against a tree and talking on his cell phone.

"Okay, listen to me carefully," I said as I turned to face Anna. I unbuttoned the top buttons on her shirt and opened it up so that her bra was showing. "Moisten your lips."

"Viviana!"

"Shh. You want him to notice you, right?"

"Yes, but I'm nervous."

"Now is not the time to be nervous. You need to be confident."

"How can I be confident when I feel like I'm about to pee on myself?" Anna crossed one leg over the other.

"Just hold on to your pee for now," I said as I tucked her hair behind her ear. "Now, listen carefully. We are both going to walk past him. When we do, I want you to turn around, make eye contact with him and mouth the words *nice butt,* and then wink at him. Then I want you to turn back around and keep walking with me."

"That doesn't make any sense. How am I supposed to talk to him if I'm walking away from him?" Anna asked, confused.

"Don't worry, once you do that, he'll catch up to us and want to get to know you," I explained.

"How do you know it will work?" she asked.

"Because I've done it at least a thousand times," I said. "Okay, you ready?"

"I'm so about to pee on myself," Anna said.

"Good, that will give you an edge," I said, marching her toward him. Anna executed the maneuver perfectly, and it only took a matter of seconds for Carlo to end his phone conversation and catch up to Anna and introduce himself.

It had gotten to be very late and the night air had turned rather chilly. I went back inside the house and upstairs to the spare room. As soon as my head landed on the pillow, I closed my eyes and went to sleep.

"Viviana." I felt my grandmother shaking my shoulder. I didn't want to wake up, but she was forcing me to.

"Viviana, get up," she said as she pulled the sheets off my body. "Come on, rise and shine."

"What time is it?" I grumbled.

"8:00 a.m."

"Ugh! Why are you waking me up so early? I wanted to sleep at least until noon," I said, perturbed.

"No, you need to get up, take a shower and put on some fresh clothes. I took them out of the dryer and brought them up."

I frowned but sat up, stretched and yawned. "Where are we going?" I asked.

"To find your mother. I want you to take me to Martin's apartment so that I can talk some sense into her."

About an hour later we pulled up in front of Martin's building on King Drive. We got out of the car and walked into the building, up the stairs and to the door of the apartment. I was surprised to see the building janitor working in the apartment.

"What's going on?" asked Grandmother Esmeralda.

"Who are you?" asked the janitor.

"I believe my daughter was staying here with a man named

Martin. Right, Viviana?" she looked at me for confirmation. I nodded yes.

"Oh, yeah. I remember seeing you around the building," the janitor said. "Well, Martin doesn't live here anymore. He was put out two days ago because he owed too much back rent."

"What?" I blurted out, not wanting to believe what I was hearing.

"Sir, do you know where they went?" asked Grandmother Esmeralda.

"I have no idea. I'm just the janitor," he explained.

"What happened to all of Martin's stuff?" I asked.

The janitor shrugged his shoulders. "I heard that a bunch of motorcycle guys rented a U-Haul and had everything packed up within a matter of an hour. These apartments are pretty small and it doesn't take long to move in or out."

"Thank you," said Grandmother Esmeralda as she turned and started walking away. "This is not good," she mumbled.

"What does this mean?" I asked, utterly confused. I pulled out my cell phone and dialed my mother's number, but my service had been cut off.

"It means that she's left you with me," said my grandmother.

"But she didn't say that she was going to do that."

"She didn't have to."

When we stepped outside I was shocked to see Toya coming down the street, approaching the building. I was glad to see that she was out of jail and I was eager to find out if she knew anything about my mother. I thought perhaps she'd seen or heard more than the janitor had.

"Wait," I said to Grandmother Esmeralda. "That's my friend coming."

"I'll wait in the car," she said as she continued toward her sedan and got in.

"Hey, Toya," I greeted her. "When did you get out?" I whispered.

"My man bailed me out. Why did you leave me like that?" Toya asked with a voice filled with hostility.

"What! Are you crazy? I wasn't about to go to jail with you," I said.

"See, it's chicks like you that I can't stand. You're not loyal. I told you not to ever cross me, didn't I?" Toya snapped. Then without warning she attacked me. Toya began pelting me with wild punches. I tried to move away from her so that I could get my wits about me and defend myself. I couldn't believe she'd just walked up on me and began throwing down. Toya knew not to let up because she knew that I'd get the better of her once she did. She grabbed my hair and started jerking on it and flung me to the ground. Before Toya could do any more damage, I heard her screaming like a puppy who'd just gotten its tail stepped on.

"I can't see!" Toya shouted as she released her grip on my hair and continued to swing wildly.

"Get up off of the ground," said Grandmother Esmeralda. I rose to my feet and noticed that Toya had her hands over her eyes, rubbing them. She couldn't stop blinking and appeared to be having a massive panic attack.

"You've burned my eyes!" she cried out.

"Let me see." Grandmother Esmeralda approached her and tried to help her.

"No, get away from me!" Toya barked and swung at my grandmother.

"Let me help you!" Grandmother Esmeralda said.

"No!" Toya stubbornly refused.

"You listen good. Go in the house and rinse your eyes with cold water. You'll live," said my grandmother. "Viviana, get in the car."

"What did you do to her?" I asked as I got in and shut the door. Before she answered me she grabbed the crucifix from around the rearview mirror and said, "Forgive me, Father. I did not mean to hurt her. Please make sure that you look after her tortured soul."

"Uhm, can we go now?" I said, feeling that perhaps other people might come to Toya's aid and turn the situation into a much bigger nightmare.

"Pepper spray. I brought it with me in case I had to use it on Martin. I didn't think that I'd have to use it on one of your friends," said Grandmother Esmeralda as she fired up the car engine and pulled off.

I rested against the seat cushion trying not to panic. How could my own mother just abandon me? I searched my mind and wondered what I'd done wrong. As we drove down the boulevard I stared out the window and pondered what would happen next.

# fourteen

*MAYA*

I glanced around the dance studio at the students in my mother's Zumba class as they waited for her to cue the music so they could begin. The health club where she taught the Saturday-morning class was packed with men and women who looked like they were excited to see one another, as well as ready to enjoy the class. Anna and I were both there because our mother had forced us to come. It wasn't like Anna and I were out of shape or dealing with teen obesity or some other horrible medical condition. It's just that my mom was a fitness maniac and wanted to make sure we took our health seriously. I'm positive that between Anna and me, we'd heard her health speech at least a million times.

"Diabetes and high blood pressure runs in the family. Take care of yourself now because no one ever says that they want to grow up to be old, sick and tired," she'd say. Both Anna and I would just let her blabber on until she ran out of gas. I, for one, knew that I'd always be thin and shapely like her. I had a very high metabolism and I healed up quickly, so my mother was really preaching to the choir when it came to me.

Now, Anna, on the other hand, loved junk food. Chocolates, cake, ice cream and anything made by Dolly Madison. Zingers and Donut Gems were her favorites. When it came to candy she loved Pixy Stix, Lemonheads and Chick-O-Sticks, Nerds, Now and Laters, taffy candy, and everything gummy. She kept a stash in her top drawer and was known to get up during the night to eat candy. Like me, Anna had a high metabolism, but she always had dental cavities. I just knew one day she was going to wake up and not have a single tooth in her head.

If you asked me, life would be so much more bearable if Anna were dropped off at an orphanage. I glanced at myself in the mirror and thought my workout gear looked perfect on me. I had on a blue-and-black Nike tank top with matching blue-and-black spa pants. I looked marvelous. Anna, being the annoying little sister that she was, copied my style. We were practically wearing the same outfit; the only difference was that her tank top was green-and-white. I wanted to choke her for trying to be chic like me.

One of the reasons I wasn't complaining too much was because I knew that Misalo was going to be at the gym. Ever since he had seen Carlo flirting with me, he had felt threatened by him. I told him that there was no need to, but my words weren't enough.

"So, you want a man with a little more muscle, aye?" he asked later that day after he had seen Carlo flirting with me at the swimming pool.

"Stop being so jealous." I tried to ease his fears, but my words offered him little comfort. Although I had to be honest with myself, if Misalo wasn't the love of my life, I'd definitely want to get to know Carlo a lot better. There was just something about him. He had swagger and the looks to go along with it. If Carlo could sing, he'd probably have girls chaining themselves to his ankles.

"Okay, guys, are you ready to Zumba!" my mother said as she adjusted her headset, which had a microphone attached to it. When she heard a chorus of voices answer she pressed the play button on the stereo remote and we began.

"We're going to work hard today, but we're going to have so much fun," she said as we all marched in place.

By the time the Zumba class was over, I was in need of a shower. When I exited the dance studio on my way to the locker room, I saw Misalo and two of his soccer-team friends over in the free-weight area. Before my mother could give me the evil eye or tell me not to go by Misalo, I was walking briskly toward him. He was lying on his back about to do the bench press. He had two giant forty-five-pound weights on each side of the bar. It looked to be way more than he could lift, but that wasn't going to stop him from trying. His friend helped him lift the bar off the rack.

"I've got it," I heard Misalo grunt the words. His friend walked to the other side of the gym.

Misalo's arms were wobbling as he held the bar above his head. I wanted to say, "Are you crazy? That's obviously too heavy," but I didn't want to startle him. I stood at a safe distance and watched him try to lower the bar to his scrawny chest. He tried to push it back up, but he couldn't. The bar fell onto his chest and rolled up toward his neck. I stood frozen with horror as I watched Misalo struggling. Just as I was about to run over and help him, Carlo appeared. He lifted the bar back up and placed it on the rack. Misalo coughed and took a few deep breaths before he sat upright.

"Thanks, but I had it," Misalo said.

"Yeah, you were about to kill yourself," Carlo said, shaking his head disapprovingly. Carlo was wearing a black tank top with dark blue gym shorts. His skin glistened with sweat from running on one of the treadmills. He looked like a god and wore his muscles proudly. For a moment I found myself wanting to place sweet kisses on his neck and nibble on his strong shoulders.

"You need to lift a lighter weight, little man," Carlo said as I walked up.

"Are you okay, Misalo?" I asked as I stood by his side.

"You didn't just see that, did you?" he asked with embarrassment in his eyes.

"Yes. Thank goodness Carlo was nearby," I said, without giving a single thought to his fragile ego.

"I didn't need the dude's help. I had it. My hands were in the wrong position. That's all," Misalo said unapologetically as he stood.

"Whatever, little hombre. You can thank me later. A word of advice, though—stick to girl weights before you try playing with the big-boy toys. Maya, it's good to see you again, baby." Carlo smiled and then winked at me. I couldn't believe that I actually felt butterflies prancing around in my belly. Carlo had eyes that I couldn't help but get lost in.

"Hey, man, Maya is my girl. I can't have you disrespecting me like that." Misalo's feathers were clearly ruffled and he wanted to fight. His soccer friends came over and stood by his side and asked what was going on.

"Guys, just calm down. Nothing is going on." I immediately tried to defuse Misalo's hostility toward Carlo. Carlo was the essence of macho. He wasn't the least bit afraid of Misalo or his friends. Carlo puckered his lips and blew me a kiss.

"Keep your damn eyes and lips off of my girl or else!" Misalo's pride was on the line and he wasn't about to back down.

"Or else what?" Carlo turned toward Misalo and called out, "Hey, Sonny and Felix, come here for a second." What neither Misalo nor I knew was that Carlo was there with his older brother, Sonny, and his cousin Felix. They were just as handsome as Carlo and had bodies that were just as sculpted. They also looked like they'd punish Misalo and his friends mercilessly if provoked. I don't know why or how Carlo's cockiness had cast its spell on me, but it had. I found myself wanting to stand behind him and press my cheeks against his back. I wanted to inhale his scent, feel the heat of his body and let him whisper sweet things in my ear. I was literally in some type of trance that I couldn't explain.

"Hello, Carlo." Anna walked up and I snapped out of my daydream. I panicked a little because I knew my mother wasn't far behind. I looked toward the dance studio and saw that she was busy talking to her students.

"Ah, *cómo estás,* Anna. It's good to see you again. Where is your cousin?" he asked.

"She went home," Anna said with a smile that was bigger than her body.

"You still haven't used the phone number I gave you,"

Anna tried to whisper, but I heard her. I rolled my eyes because Carlo was so out of her league.

"Guys, look." I finally found my voice. "We just have a big misunderstanding here. No harm has been done. Anna, we should go before Mom comes," I said, wanting her to step away from Carlo.

"Mom is busy," Anna said defiantly.

"Anna, I'm not playing with you," I said a little more aggressively.

"Wait a minute. This cute little woman here is your sister?" Carlo asked.

"Oh, Carlo." Anna giggled uncontrollably. She obviously had a ridiculously huge crush on Carlo.

"Beauty runs in the family I see." Carlo smiled. At that moment, the worst thing in the world happened. My mother walked over. I wanted to go and stick my head in the ground.

"Ladies, what's going on?" my mother asked as she looked at Misalo and his friends and then at Carlo and his crew. When she took a glance at Carlo, she flinched a little as if she had to make sure that her eyes were not lying to her.

"Is this your mother?" Carlo asked me.

"Yes," Anna answered before I could.

"Respect, señorita." Carlo, his brother, and cousin nodded their heads in a show of respect to my mother. "You have beautiful daughters. If Maya continues to hang around guys like him—" he pointed to Misalo "—she'll get into trouble. He has a very short temper. I have two sisters. They're only nine and eleven, but since I'm their big brother I make sure they know not to hang around boys with tempers." I couldn't believe how easily and smoothly Carlo had tossed Misalo in front of a big-ass bus.

"Why are you talking to Misalo when your father and I have asked you not to?" My mother started in on me.

"Mrs. Rogers, I wanted to apologize for—" My mother tossed up her hand and made Misalo talk to it. I glanced at him. I could see the humiliation taking over his prideful heart.

"Come on, fellas. Let's go," Carlo said and politely excused himself. I watched Anna communicate with Carlo through her eyes. She wanted him to call her so badly. I once again got lost in Carlo's swagger.

"Don't look at him, look at me!" My mother popped her fingers in front of my eyes.

"I'm sorry. What were you saying?" I asked.

"I'm going to go, Maya. I'll see you around," Misalo said. I craned my neck in his direction, but he'd already begun to walk away, with his head slumped between his shoulders.

"Mom, I didn't know he was here," I explained as feelings of regret filled my heart. I was utterly confused by everything that had just happened. I didn't know how to explain any of it. I thought my mother would be angrier, but she wasn't.

"When you're ready to talk about all of this, just let me know," she said.

"Talk about all of what?" I asked, trying to pretend that I was completely ignorant.

"Don't play dumb with me, Maya. I've had feelings like that, too, and I know everything you're thinking. You're confused and you don't know what to do." I wanted to deny that she was right but I couldn't. I glanced at Anna, who still had her eyes focused on Carlo as he entered the locker room.

"You need to talk to Anna," I said, throwing her in front of a train so that my mother wouldn't focus on me so hard. "I think she's trying to date."

"I am not!" My words got Anna's attention.

"Oh, God. Don't tell me that you both like the same boy?" My mother sounded disappointed.

"I don't like Carlo," I quickly said. My mother gave me a look that said she didn't believe a word I'd just said.

"You need to talk to Maya about all of the secret rendez-vous she's been having with Misalo. She's not staying away from him like you and Dad have asked," Anna said. I looked at her and lowered my eyes to slits. That was to let her know that at some point I was going to get even with her for mentioning that.

When we arrived back home, my father and brother were in the family room listening to music. My brother, Paul, had made the mistake of asking my father how to slow dance. This was something he should've asked my mother.

"Raven, come down here so we can show this boy how to dance the right way," my father yelled up the staircase from the basement.

"Herman, I'm tired," my mother answered back as she walked into the kitchen.

"It will only take a minute. He has some girl he's trying to impress," my father said. Both Anna and I found that to be humorous and laughed loudly. Our little brother was such a video game nerd. The last thing that Anna or I ever thought we'd see him with was a girl.

"Oh, you guys think that's funny?" my mother asked as she removed a chilled bottle of water from the refrigerator.

"Yes," Anna and I both said as we kept laughing and making fun of our little brother.

"Come on. Everyone downstairs." My mother directed us toward the basement and family room. When we came down, our father had moved all of the furniture against the walls so there was plenty of space to dance. He and Paul were in the center of the floor, where Dad was trying to teach him how to move his feet.

"Come on, Paul. You're moving like you have two left feet," Dad complained.

"I'm trying, but my feet don't work that way," Paul said. Anna and I snickered as we found a place to sit.

"Herman, your girls also need a birds-and-bees lesson," my mother said.

"Huh?" Dad asked. I immediately stopped laughing, because the last thing I wanted was to have a conversation like that as a group activity.

"It appears as if all of our children are suddenly interested in romance," my mother announced.

"I only wanted to know how to dance and look cool," my brother quickly said.

"And why do you want to look cool?" my mother asked.

Paul shrugged his shoulders. "I don't know. Just to look cool."

"No. It's because you want to get attention from girls." My mother didn't buy Paul's line of bull for even an instant. My mother took a seat on the love chair. "So, tell our children what romance is like." My father opened his mouth but no words came out. I could tell that he was searching for what he should say.

"Wow, I'm really on the spot, aren't I?" my father said.

"Yes, you are. Tell them how you romanced me. Why don't you start there," my mother said. Although I'd heard the story before, I never grew tired of hearing it.

"Well, I met your mother when I was twenty-four years old and she was twenty. We were both in our second year of college and I was the most handsome man on campus," Dad boasted, but everyone knew that wasn't true. My mother laughed.

"You were cute, but you needed the touch of a woman." Mom laughed.

"Don't listen to your mother, girls. I was a suave man fresh out of the military, and I had the moves, the looks and—"

My mother interrupted him. "No money and no car. Your father was a disciplined man and he—"

"Do you want to tell this story or are you going to let me tell it?" My father broke up my mother's version of events.

"Go on." She waved him off.

"True, I didn't have much money or a car, but I had heart."

"So, get to the part about how you guys met," said my little brother as he sat on the floor next to my mother.

"Well, your mother was a cheerleader and was the best dancer on the squad. She could move like no other girl on the team. Whenever she danced she stood out from the crowd. She was whipping her hair back and forth long before Willow Smith was born. I went to all of the basketball and football games just to watch her perform."

"Your father and his friends made a habit of hanging

around begging girls for their phone numbers like sailors on shore leave. The only reason they were near us was because of our revealing outfits. We showed a lot of skin," my mother added.

My father laughed. "Oh, yeah, because she had this one white outfit that hugged her body like a glove and—"

"Herman, they get the picture." My mother caught him before he got too caught up in the memory.

My father smiled again. "Anyway, at the time she was dating one of the football players, and I was doing my best to steal her away from him."

"Wait, you mean that Mom had a boyfriend and you took her from him?" asked Paul, who seemed to believe that this was an important historical news flash he'd missed.

"He was no good for her, son. She didn't know it at the time, but I did. She was my woman, my soul mate, and I wasn't going to allow her to get away from me," my father said with pride.

"So, how did you take her from the other guy?" Paul continued with his questions.

"Well, as luck would have it, the following semester your mom and I ended up in the same chemistry class. I made sure that she wound up being my lab partner."

"Your father *insisted* that I become his partner," my mother once again interjected.

"I knew a lot about chemistry and didn't want to see her struggling with the class, so I offered to help her with her studies. We ended up spending a lot of time together." Dad smiled at the memory.

"Well, what about her boyfriend? Didn't he get mad?" Paul asked.

"Oh, yes, he got very angry and extremely jealous if I remember correctly," my father said, glancing over at my mother.

"Yes, he was," she admitted.

"Anyway, she didn't know it, but I was secretly talking to her girlfriends who didn't like the guy she was dating. They were telling me all of the things that she liked and didn't like. So by having the inside scoop, I knew I'd be able to win her over."

"Wow, that is so special," I said as I tucked my legs beneath me.

"But, Dad, wasn't that disrespectful?" Paul asked.

"All is fair in love and war," said my Dad.

"Huh?" Paul was completely clueless.

"I didn't take her, son. I was a total gentleman during those days. I treated your mother like a queen. Her boyfriend, on the other hand, well, that's another story." My father turned to my mother.

"Yes. The guy I was dating and thought I was in love with turned out to be a real monster," said my mother.

"What did he do?" asked Paul.

"He was an abusive guy. At the beginning of our relationship he would tell me that his jealousy was a sign of his love for me. Then he started questioning who I was with during the day and who I had been talking to."

"Then his suspicions were right, because you were talking to Dad," Paul pointed out.

"At that time your father and I weren't romantically involved at all. We were just friends. But my boyfriend at the time had been acting this way long before your father came around. He'd accuse me of flirting with other men when we'd go out, which of course, I wasn't. Then it got to the point that he didn't want me to ever leave his side because he feared that I'd meet someone and leave him. He'd call all of the time and come to my dorm unannounced. He was very insecure and I stupidly tried to change him."

"So, you guys kept dating?" asked Paul.

"Yes," my mother answered.

"I'd hoped they'd break up, but your mother hung in there with him. I think she believed he was going to get drafted into the NFL and she'd marry him and live a life of luxury."

"No, I didn't," my mother disputed that claim.

"That's not what your girlfriends told me," Dad countered.

"They were just nosy gossip girls," Mom said, not giving any weight or validity to their perception of her during that time period.

"Right after our graduation ceremony in spring of 1990, I got her alone and told her how I truly felt about her," said my father.

"By that time your father had become a very dear friend. I had feelings for him, but I was torn because I also had feelings for my boyfriend, in spite of all his flaws," Mom said.

"Your mother left me holding my heart in my hand," said my father. "And, Paul, let me tell you. It's not easy for a guy to watch the woman he loves walk away."

"Why did you break his heart, Mom?" Paul turned to look at her.

"His heart wasn't that broken," she said.

"Yes, it was," my father said. "A few weeks later I was called up for duty."

"That's when you went to the Gulf War, right?" I asked.

"Yup. I was shipped off to Texas, where I did some specialized training with chemical weapons. I had to do another two years in the military before I was able to get out. When I finally got out, I moved to Chicago and stayed with relatives until I got a job and my own place."

"Oh, here comes the good part," Anna said.

My father chuckled. "I was out one night with some military buddies who had taken me to a dance club where bachata dance competitions were held. Of all the places your mother could have walked into, that night she walked into that one. She was with her sister, Salena, and they were both dressed to kill. Once they sat down, I sent a drink over to their table. When the waitress pointed to me to show your mother who the drink had come from, she couldn't believe that I was there. When I looked into her eyes they sparkled like diamonds."

"That is so romantic." I sighed.

"Your father surprised me," my mother said, picking up the story. "I never expected to see him again. The first thing I asked him when he came over was if he was still single. I was happy beyond words when he said that he was."

"So, the guy from college, what happened to him?" Paul asked.

"She'd broken up with him—duh!" Anna said, poking fun at Paul.

"A bachata song came on and I asked your mother to dance with me," my dad explained.

"I was very nervous, because the Herman that I knew in college did not know how to dance at all. So I told him that he shouldn't embarrass himself."

"Oh, I got your mother real good that night. I pulled her out of her seat and walked her onto the dance floor. I told her to make sure she kept up." My father met my mother's gaze, and I could still see the love in his eyes that he had for her.

"Your father didn't tell me that while he was in Texas he'd learned a lot about Mexican culture, dance, music and everything."

"Your mother forgot that before I was in college I spent four years in the military traveling around the world. I'd been to Spain, Japan and Africa. I learned as much about other cultures as I could."

"So there I was, standing on the dance floor with my sister, Salena, glaring at me as if I'd lost my mind," said my mother.

"Come here, baby. Let's show them how to bachata," said my father.

"My feet hurt," my mother whined.

"I'll rub them when we're done."

"Go on and do it," I said, getting up and placing their favorite dance CD, which contained the song they danced to, in the stereo. I pressed Play and took a seat. My father slowly grooved to the rhythm of the melody being played by a Spanish guitar. My mother joined him. They took each other's hands and began to dance. Their bachata dance was filled with spins, turns and lots of hip movement by both partners. I enjoyed watching my parents dance with each other. They'd been together for so long that they knew each other's moves. Even though they hadn't practiced, they moved with flawless precision. They smiled at each other, they laughed with each other and they enjoyed each other. My heart started to swell. I wanted to have a romantic marriage just like theirs.

Later that evening I ran an errand with my mother. While we walked around the grocery store she got a phone call from my grandmother.

"What do you mean Salena has disappeared?" my mother said as I stood near her and listened with great interest.

"Viviana has no idea where she could be?" she asked.

I could hear my grandmother's muffled voice say, "No."

"Why would Salena just leave like that? It doesn't make any sense," my mother said. She was clearly getting upset as we moved down the aisle where all the bread was shelved.

"Who got into a fight?" my mother asked. I glanced over at her because I wanted to know, as well.

"What do you mean you got into a fight?" She stopped walking and so did I.

"Mama, you should've called the police. You can't allow Viviana to drag you into her drama." My mother paused as my grandmother spoke. "I know you're too old to be fighting." My mother paused again as my grandmother spoke to her.

"Mom, I'll have to talk to Herman about having Viviana stay with us. I just can't spring this on him all of a sudden." I got involved at that moment. I stood in front of my mother and got her attention and whispered loudly.

"I don't want Viviana to come live with us," I said with a grave sense of urgency before she agreed to do anything.

"Mom, Viviana has a reputation and she..." My mother paused yet again. "I know your health isn't the best and I know you're on a fixed income. You don't have to remind me.

"I'll talk to Herman tonight about it," my mother said. I walked away at that moment, because I knew that Grandmother Esmeralda was going to win and Viviana was coming to stay with us for an indefinite length of time.

# fifteen

VIVIANA

MY life really sucks. Not only has my own mother walked out on me, but now my grandmother is shipping me off to live under the same roof with the one person I can hardly get along with—Maya. My grandmother had somehow convinced my aunt Raven to take me in until my mother decided to surface. Although I would be staying with family who had known me all of my life, I still felt as if I were intruding. I also knew that the only reason I was being taken in was because my grandmother wasn't going to have it any other way.

When I arrived back at Maya's house and Aunt Raven met me at the door, she gave me a kiss on the cheek and a big hug.

"You're welcome to stay for as long as necessary," she said. Although her words were kind and probably genuine, I still felt like the pile of steaming dinosaur crap that had suddenly materialized in the middle of the room.

"Where will I be sleeping, the garage?" I asked sarcastically.

"No, honey, why would you think we'd place you out in the cold garage?" Aunt Raven asked.

"I don't know," I said, feeling really vulnerable.

"Anna insisted that you sleep in her bedroom with her," she informed me. I perked up a little. I really liked that girl. "She has a queen-size bed that you guys can share until we can figure out what's going on."

"Is Anna here?" I asked.

"Yes. Just go on upstairs. You know where to find her." I gave my aunt another hug before I headed up to Anna's room.

Grandmother Esmeralda decided to stay for a few days until I got settled in. If the truth were to be told, she only stayed because she knew that my being there was putting a lot of pressure on Aunt Raven. It was an unsettling feeling knowing that I was the cause of underlying tension in the house.

While Aunt Raven and Uncle Herman were at work, Grandmother Esmeralda took it upon herself to make sure no major fallouts happened. Anna and I got along well, Maya stayed to herself and Paul got lost in his video games. Although Aunt Raven told her not to, Grandmother Esmeralda did all the laundry, cleaning and cooking for several days. Coming home to a clean house and a hot meal was something that went over well with Uncle Herman.

I received a text message from an old friend who lived in my old neighborhood. He made money on the side as a DJ at parties and said that he was throwing a summer bash and was inviting everyone he knew. I got the address from him, but was a little disappointed when I realized that it was in the city.

"Damn," I whispered to myself as I stood in the bathroom and read his text. If I were still living with my mother and Martin I could come and go at will. I knew that in order to go I'd have to get really creative and do a lot of scheming to pull it off without getting caught. After thinking about it for a day, I came up with a plan. It was a risky one, but I was willing to give it a try, because I totally needed to blow off some steam and have some fun for once in my life. I decided that it was best to keep my plans all to myself. The less everyone knew, the better. I figured I'd just sneak out of the house for a few hours and come back in. Aunt Raven had already given me a spare door key and the alarm code for the house. I could exit the house through a side door in the basement, where Grandmother Esmeralda was sleeping on the sofa bed. She slept like a corpse so I knew she wouldn't hear anything. I figured I'd take her car keys and drive myself down to the party. I'd see some old friends, have a good time and be back before anyone noticed that I was gone.

On the night of the party I placed the clothes I'd change into in the trunk of Grandmother Esmeralda's car. I waited until 11:30 p.m. when everyone was sound asleep. Once I got out of the house, I was about to get into Grandmother Esmeralda's car, which was parked in the driveway, when I heard someone say, "Where the hell are you going?"

I thought for sure I'd gotten busted by my aunt. I closed my eyes tightly and nervously turned in the direction of the voice, hoping I could come up with a damn good lie.

"Are you sneaking out of our house?" I opened my eyes and realized that it was Maya and not Aunt Raven asking the questions. Sometimes they could sound like each other. Maya was sitting on the front porch on the swing.

"Keep your voice down," I said as I moved toward her.

"Were you about to take Grandmother Esmeralda's car?" Maya asked.

"I've taken it before and returned it. It's no big deal," I said.

"You don't even have a driver's license," Maya said.

"A lot of people don't have a license or insurance, but does that keep them from driving around and getting them to where they need to go?" I asked.

"And exactly where are you going?" she asked.

"None of your business. Besides, what are you doing out here this late?" I whispered softly.

"I couldn't sleep so I came out for some air," Maya explained.

"It sounds like you're freaking bored to death." Maya didn't deny what I'd just said. "I'm going out to a party," I reluctantly informed her.

"You can't just go to a party without asking." Maya was starting to sound like someone's mother.

"Yes, I can. I always come and go as I please without anyone's permission, and I'm not about to start asking for it now," I said indignantly.

"I'm telling." Maya rose to her feet to go squeal.

"If you go in there and say something, I'll deny everything and lie on you. I'll say that I came out to the car to get my purse and saw you out here with Misalo."

"That's a lie! Misalo wasn't here. My parents wouldn't believe you," Maya said.

"How do your parents know that you're telling the truth? After all, you did get busted with him in your room. It would be my word against yours. Besides, I'm still in my pajamas. Why would I go to a party in my pj's?" I gambled with my last comment, hoping Maya was the perfect princess that I knew she was, and had never in her life snuck out of the house and stashed a change of clothes somewhere. Maya was silent for a moment. Then to my utter shock she asked, "Where is this party at?"

"Oh, hell no! Don't tell me you want to go," I said.

"I'm feeling daring, so either you take me or the minute you pull off, I'll wake up everyone in the house and let them know that you've disappeared...just like your mother," Maya said.

I wanted to choke her for bringing up my mother like that. I was about to drop the entire idea of going to the party and just beat Maya up, when a mean-spirited thought entered my mind. It would be the perfect way to get Maya into some really hot water.

"Okay. I'll take you," I agreed. "How long will it take you to get ready, because we don't have much time. We've got to get there, have our fun and then come back. I want to be back in the house at about 3:30 a.m."

"It won't take me long at all," Maya said.

"I'll be in the car." I smiled because she had no clue what I was about to do to her.

Maya got dressed in ten minutes and I drove us to the address as quickly as I could. During the drive there I acted as if everything would be fine and assured Maya that she'd have a great time. When we arrived at the address and entered the house, the party was alive and buzzing with energy. The music was hot, people were dancing and the drinks were flowing. It didn't take me long to run into several people that I knew. A friend gave me a can of beer and I offered one to Maya. I purposely didn't introduce her to anyone there. I wanted her to feel totally lost and friendless. Almost immediately, I could tell that she regretted the decision to come. Knowing that brought me a twisted kind of joy. I raised my can high in the air and screamed. Several friends joined me as I rocked and grooved my way to another section of the house, leaving Maya, the human wallflower, behind.

During all of my excitement I stumbled across several people who were pretty wasted. I took the opportunity to pick their pockets. I grabbed a plastic bag out of the kitchen and went to work. It was so easy. I took jewelry and cash. About two hours after we'd arrived I went looking for Maya. I was actually a little disappointed that she wasn't searching for me. When I found her and saw what she was doing, my jaw hit the floor.

"What were the odds of that happening? *That's* why she hasn't been looking for me," I muttered to myself as I watched Maya sharing a slow dance with Carlo. If someone had come and told me that Maya was all hugged up with Carlo I would've called them a liar, but there they were, all hugged up.

"Unbelievable," I murmured as I removed my cell phone and set it to video mode. I stood in a corner and filmed it, knowing that at some point the video clip would be very useful. Once I'd seen enough, I placed the nail in Maya's coffin, and left her stranded at the party.

# sixteen

*MAYA*

In the back of my mind I was hoping that by showing Viviana that I was a bit daring I would earn a little credibility with her and we'd be able to get closer and squash the animosity that existed between us. I tried to ease the tension by attempting to talk to her in the car during the drive over, even though I was a nervous wreck. My biggest fear was that we'd get pulled over by the cops and end up in jail for joyriding. Thankfully, even with Viviana's less than perfect driving, we made it to the party without incident. As we entered the house I thought we'd get a chance to really settle down a little, enjoy our little adventure, and be able to talk about it fondly when we were old and had children of our own. Instead, nothing happened the way I'd envisioned it would. I couldn't believe Viviana just disappeared on me the moment we arrived. I didn't know anyone there and a lot of the people who were there looked too old to be teenagers. I was clearly in over my head and had no idea where I was. One guy, who looked old enough to be my father, came up to me said, "Well, aren't you a pretty little thing. Do you like older men?" I immediately got away from him because he gave me the creeps. I searched for Viviana, but I couldn't find her because there were so many people crammed into such a tight space. I began to panic as I flashed back to the last party I'd been to with Misalo, where I broke my leg. I pushed my way through the crowd and made it out to the backyard, where there was more room. I searched and searched for Viviana, but I didn't see her. Feeling as if I'd made the blunder of a lifetime, I pulled out my cell phone and called Keysha. I hoped and prayed that she had her phone near, because I really needed to talk to her.

"Hello?" Keysha sounded like a frog croaking on its lily pad.

"Keysha, wake up!" I urged her to come completely alive.

"Who is this?" she asked, still drifting between sleep and reality.

"Keysha, wake up!" I shouted into the phone.

"Stop yelling at me. Who is this? Mom, is this you?" Keysha thought I was her mother.

"No, it's me, Maya," I said.

"Maya? Girl, what time is it?" she asked.

"It's two o'clock in the morning," I said.

"Oh, wow. What's the matter? You can't sleep again?" Keysha knew me well, but she was going to really freak out when I told her where I was and what I'd done.

"No. I'm at a party," I said.

"A party?" I could tell that Keysha was completely awake. "How come you didn't tell me there was a party tonight?"

"I didn't find out about it until around midnight," I said.

"Midnight? What are you talking about, Maya?"

"Are you totally awake yet?"

"Yeah, I'm sitting up in the bed now. I've just turned on the light. Now, what's up?"

"Oh, Keysha, I've really, really messed up," I said, panic-stricken.

"What did you do?" she asked.

"I snuck out of the house to come to a party with Viviana and now I think she's left me here." I wanted to cry, but I held on to my tears.

"Why in the world did you sneak out of the house with Viviana? You know that girl doesn't like you."

"I thought by doing this we'd somehow grow close, but I was totally wrong," I said.

"Okay, calm down. Let me think for a moment." Keysha paused. "How did you get there?"

"Viviana took my grandmother's car keys and we drove here," I explained.

"And she left you there?" Keysha asked, making certain of my situation.

"Yes."

"Where is the party at?" she asked.

"Somewhere in the city," I said.

"Are you serious?"

"Yes, I am. Viviana seriously left me here stranded. Oh, God, if my parents find out what I've done, they're going to shoot me. I wouldn't be surprised if Viviana's back at the house right now sounding the alarm that I'm missing. Why did I ever trust that girl?" I said as I hit my forehead several times with the heel of my hand.

"Okay. Just relax. First, you need to figure out where you

are. Then you'll have to call a cab, because public transportation is just too dangerous this time of night."

"Keysha, I don't have any money on me."

"You're joking, right?"

"No. I'm not working, remember?" I reminded her that I'd lost my job. Keysha released a giant sigh.

"Okay, here is what we'll do. Call a cab and I'll have the driver bring you home. I have one hundred dollars in cash. When you get close to home, call me and I'll sneak out of the house and come over to your place so I can pay your fare."

"Keysha, I can't have you sneaking out of the house for me." I felt horribly guilty.

"Well, you can't come over here and knock on the door, either," she said. I'd just about given in to the idea that her plan was my best and only option. That's when I saw Carlo walking toward me.

"Oh, my God!" I said.

"What? Maya, what's wrong?" Keysha asked nervously.

"Carlo is here," I said.

"Carlo?"

"Yeah," I answered her. Carlo approached me with a giant grin on his face.

"You're the last person on earth I ever expected to see here," he said.

"That makes two of us," I said as I swallowed hard. "Say, you didn't happen to drive here, did you?" I asked.

"Yeah, I did. Why?" Carlo answered.

"Do you think I could get a ride back home with you?" I practically begged him.

"Sure, I wasn't leaving just yet, though," he said.

"Keysha." I spoke into my phone.

"Yeah, I'm here."

"I'll call you back. Carlo is going to give me a ride home," I said.

"Maya," Keysha called to me.

"Yeah."

"Are you sure about getting a ride home with Carlo?" I could hear the concern in her voice.

"Yes. It will be fine. I'll call you when I get back in the house," I said, ending the call.

I explained my situation to Carlo and begged him to take me home. "I'll be forever indebted to you," I said.

"What's in it for me?" he asked.

"Huh? What do you mean?" I asked, confused.

"What do I get for taking you home?" he asked.

"I'm not giving you any booty, Carlo. I'd rather call my father and deal with him than to do that," I said without flinching.

"No, silly, I wasn't thinking of anything that extreme. I was thinking of something more along the lines of a dance. You're without question the prettiest girl here and it would be a dream come true if I could share at least one dance with you."

"Well, I don't see any harm in that," I said.

"Good. I happen to know the DJ. There is a song in particular that I want to dance to," he said. "Come on, follow me."

Carlo had his friend play a popular romantic song. I hesitantly stepped into Carlo's embrace and danced with him. He placed one hand on the small of my back and held on to my other hand. Carlo moved sensually and I forced myself to keep my eyes off his hips. I looked up and met his gaze.

"You have pretty eyes. They shine like moonlight shimmering on water," Carlo whispered. I didn't know what to say. His words were so romantic and it was all too easy to get lost in the moment. I told myself to hold it together. I forced myself to think of Misalo, but his image vanished when Carlo began to sing in my ear.

"Oh, God. You know how to sing, too," I said as I surrendered to his sweet words and the melody of his voice.

Carlo held true to his word and drove me home safely. When we arrived, I saw that Grandmother Esmeralda's car was sitting in the driveway, which meant that Viviana had purposely left me.

"Oh, I'm going to make her pay dearly for this," I muttered as Carlo put the car in Park.

"So, do you think I'll ever get a chance to dance and sing to you again?" he asked. I exhaled and smiled nervously.

"I don't think that's such a good idea," I said, "but we can be friends." Carlo licked his lips.

"You want to be so much more than my friend," he said confidently. I didn't know what to say to that, so I said nothing.

"Look, I'd better go, it's very late. I'll see you around, okay?"

"Sure," he said. I gave Carlo a kiss on the cheek and exited his car.

I was able to enter the house through a side door, the same side door that Viviana had crept out of the house through. The entrance led to the laundry room. Once inside, I removed my street clothes, put them in the laundry basket and grabbed from the dryer some fresh pajamas that Grandmother Esmeralda hadn't yet folded up. I purposely messed up my hair so that I didn't look as if I'd just come in from a party. As I was making my way to my bedroom, I ran into my grandmother, who was coming out of the bathroom.

She screamed and jumped when she saw me, "My God, Maya. You nearly gave me a heart attack. What are you doing down here?"

"Uhm…" I paused as I tried to think of a quick lie. "I came down to look for some extra bedsheets."

"Come on, Maya, you came in from outside, didn't you?" she asked and I tried not to panic.

"No," I lied. "I'm seriously cold and—"

"I'm just kidding," she said.

I put a fake smile on my face, hugged her briefly and rushed upstairs. Once I made it to my bedroom I sent Keysha a text message to let her know that I'd made it home safely.

I didn't awake until early in the afternoon the next day. I took a deep breath and then exhaled as I threaded my fingers through my hair and away from my face. I didn't get out of bed right away; instead I listened for the sounds of activity. Hearing none, I sat upright, stretched my arms high above my head and yawned.

"What a night," I murmured as I stood and headed toward the bathroom. Once I'd freshened up, I went downstairs and headed directly toward the kitchen because I was hungry.

"It's about time you woke up," said my mother. She was stepping down off a ladder.

"What are you doing?" I asked.

"Washing the windows. I had to use a ladder to get up top," she said.

"Where is Grandma?" I asked.

"She's gone home. I love her dearly, but she was driving me crazy with all of the cleaning she was doing. No matter how many times I told her that I didn't want her to clean the house she wouldn't listen. So today I've decided to really do some detailed work. Do you want to help?"

I looked at my mother oddly. I guess the look on my face said it all.

"You live here, too, you know. Your father and I are going to get much more strict on you guys about your chores. After I'm done, there will be no more sneaking off to bed with a pile of dishes in the sink. There will be no more unfolded laundry piled up on the sofa and there will be—"

I interrupted her, "Mom, I'm not messy like Paul and Anna. I keep my room spotless. I'm always telling them they need to clean up their messes, but they just look at me as if I'm trying to boss them around," I griped.

"Well, from now on, especially since Viviana is here for God only knows how long, a lot of things are going to change."

"Speaking of that heifer, where is she?" I didn't mean to call Viviana out of her name.

"Maya. Don't speak of her like that!" My mother wasn't pleased with my attitude toward her, but if she only knew what Viviana had done she'd feel differently. As much as I wanted to tell her everything, a larger part of me wanted revenge.

"Sorry. Where is she?" I asked.

"She, Anna and Paul are all at the pool. Your grandmother took the liberty of spending what little spare money she had to buy Viviana a new bathing suit. Your father and I have been arguing about taking on the additional financial responsibility for Viviana."

"You guys aren't getting a divorce over this, are you?" I asked.

"Not yet," my mother muttered.

"What does that mean?" I asked.

"It means that you shouldn't worry about that. Your father and I will work through this."

Speaking slowly I said, "So Salena still hasn't surfaced at all?"

"No. Salena has been flaky all of her life," Mom said as she started cleaning the glass on the cabinets. "She's just never been able to get her crap together." I wanted to tell my mother what I had overheard Salena say about her when I was staying with my grandmother, but I didn't think now was a good time to bring that up.

"Do you mind if I go out to the pool?" I asked.

"No, just make sure everyone is back here in time for dinner."

"I will. Oh, and Mom, you don't have to worry about cleaning up my room."

"Oh, I'm not going that far with my cleaning. Well, I will go and pull the sheets off of Anna's bed and get them washed up, but that's about it. I'm not going to get into the habit of cleaning your rooms." I gave my mother a big hug and told her that I loved her.

"Aren't you going to eat first?" she asked.

"You know that you shouldn't eat before getting in the pool," I playfully reminded her.

"Fine, that's on you," she said and continued on with her detailed cleaning.

When I arrived at the pool I went and stood next to Keysha, who was standing at the edge of the swimming pool with a whistle in her mouth. She was monitoring a group of fifth-grade kids who were playing roughly.

"Hey, girl," I greeted her.

"What's up?" Keysha said and then blew her whistle. "No splashing!" she growled at one of the boys, who immediately apologized. "Ugh! These little boys are working my nerves."

"Where are you sitting?" I asked.

"Over there, in the chair next to the table where the sign-in sheet is." She pointed with her index finger.

"Have you seen Anna and my cousin Viviana?" I asked.

"Yeah, over there in that far corner." Keysha nodded in their direction. I glanced over at Viviana and she mockingly waved at me.

"I am going to crack her damn skull open!" I said, dropping my beach bag and marching toward Viviana. Rage just consumed me, and all I wanted to do was get her back for what she'd done. I'd almost reached Viviana when Keysha grabbed my arm by the wrist and jerked me to a stop.

"Hold on, Maya. As much as I want you to beat her down, it's going to have to wait," she said.

"No, Keysha, she's got it coming and you know it!" I raised my voice. Keysha maneuvered around me and was now standing directly in front of me. "If you do this right here and now, you're going to force me to either join the fight or break it up. If I join it, then you know your little sister is going to get involved and I don't want to beat up my best friend's little sister. If I break it up, then I'm going to have to kick you out, and I don't want to do that, either."

"Keysha, get out of my way," I said, trying to step around her. I could see that Viviana had risen to her feet and was tying up her hair in anticipation of a fight.

"Let her go, Keysha," Viviana said, provoking me.

"Come on, Maya, please. Don't do this here," Keysha begged.

"Then kick her out!" I snapped. I noticed how other people at the pool were paying attention to the drama unfolding.

"She hasn't done anything. If I kick her out for no reason, you know your sister will show her how to file a complaint against me. You know the rules, Maya." Keysha now had both of her hands firmly on my shoulders and was controlling my movements.

"Fine!" I snarled. "I live with her. I'll see her later on and deal with her then. Now, let me go," I said.

"Are you sure you're cool?" Keysha asked.

"I'm cool," I said. When she released me I walked to the other side of the pool, removed my cutoff blue jean shorts and T-shirt, then got situated on a lawn chair. I took out a fashion magazine I'd brought along and started thumbing through it. About an hour later, Misalo entered the pool with his friends. I was happy to see him, even though I had not spoken to him since I'd last seen him at the gym.

"Hi, baby," I said, reaching out my arms, expecting to give him a hug and a nice passionate kiss. But Misalo just stepped away from me and sat down in the chair next to me.

"What's that all about?" I asked, feeling very offended.

"I don't know, Maya, you tell me. What is it all about?" he asked. Misalo was clearly angry with me, but I had no clue what I'd done to make him so upset.

"What are you talking about?" I said, attempting to charm him with my pretty smile.

"You've really pissed me off, that's what's up." If looks could kill Misalo would have shot me down right then and there.

"Don't use that kind of language with me," I warned.

"Oh, now you're going to tell me how to express my own freaking anger? You know what, Maya, go screw yourself!"

I snapped at him. "Who do you think you're talking to?"

"You!" Misalo said, not backing down.

"Okay, what could I have possibly done to make you this angry?" I sat up and then turned to face him.

"The way you treated me at the gym, Maya. You treated me like I was an annoying fly buzzing around your picnic basket."

"No, I didn't," I disagreed.

"And Carlo. I see the way you look at him. You're thirsting after him. Are you seeing him behind my back or something?"

"Baby, no. Not at all. Carlo means nothing to me," I said, taking his hand into my own.

"Could have fooled me—even your mother looked like she wanted a piece of him," Misalo continued.

"Leave my mother out of this," I said, giving him a second warning.

"Why are you doing this to us? Don't you understand how much I love you?" Misalo asked. I could tell his heart was very wounded.

"I'm not doing anything, baby," I said, trying to get him to believe that my words were true.

"You haven't even called me, Maya. What's that about?" He asked a legitimate question to which I responded, "You wouldn't believe how crazy the past few days have been. My cousin Viviana has moved in with us because her mother abandoned her. So, I've been dealing with all of that drama. I'm sorry for neglecting my boo. Can you find it in your heart to forgive me?" I asked as I rubbed his thighs with my hands.

"I don't know." He crossed his arms and glared at me hard, as if he thought I was lying.

"Please?" I begged as I craned my neck up to meet his lips. I paused briefly to make sure he wouldn't move. Then I gave him the most passionate kiss I could summon.

Viviana and Anna eventually left, which I was all too pleased about. I had no clue as to where they were going and I didn't care. Misalo and I got hungry, so he told his friends that he'd catch up with them later. I told Keysha I'd call her later and fill her in. After that, I left the pool to spend the rest of the afternoon with Misalo addressing his insecurities and jealousy. Since Misalo had the car, we drove over to Country Club Hills and got something to eat at Sonic Drive-In. Afterward, Misalo and I headed over to the movie theater to see what was playing.

*"Beastly,"* he said, reading the marquee.

"We should see that. I hear it's a romantic movie." I looped my arm around his and rested my head against his shoulder.

"You sure that's what you want to see?" he asked.

"I'm positive," I said as I kissed him on the cheek.


I barely made it home in time for dinner, as my mother had requested. Not that it would have mattered, because all hell was breaking loose when I arrived. Apparently, while my mother was in Anna's room she ran across a bag of Viviana's that had what appeared to be stolen jewelry and a small amount of pot in it. When I walked in, I had to listen to the "just say no to drugs" speech just like everyone else. When my mother was done I walked up to Viviana and said, "You'd better grow eyes in the back of your head because I haven't forgotten what you did."

"Back up off of me, Maya. I'm not in the freaking mood!" Viviana issued a threat of her own.

"I don't care what mood you're in, trick! You'd better walk lightly and sleep with your damn eyes open," I said and then pushed her. I was ready to fight right then and there. I was ready to roll and rumble and deal with the consequences afterward. However, I was befuddled when Viviana refused to defend herself and fight back. I looked into her eyes, which were filling with tears.

"I don't feel sorry for you!" I barked and was about to kick her when Anna stepped in front of me.

"Leave her alone, Maya. Mom came down on her pretty hard before you got here about bringing pot into the house."

"As she should have! If it were me I'd kick you out of my house." My words were merciless.

Anna pushed me away. "Maya, seriously. Leave her alone."

# seventeen

VIVIANA

The following morning when I awoke I had a massive cramp in my neck and back, from sleeping on the sofa bed in the basement. I stood up and stretched my body in an effort to work out the kinks. Now that Grandmother Esmeralda was gone I was sleeping on the sofa bed, but I didn't know how many more nights I could take with a metal bar stabbing me in my back. I went to the bathroom, flipped the light switch, stood in front of the mirror and ran some water. I opened the cupboard and retrieved a fresh facecloth.

I was really messed up emotionally after Aunt Raven had gone off on me about the stolen jewelry that I picked up at the party. She nailed everyone for it with an all-family drug talk, but I knew that her comments were really meant for me. I was totally ready to own up to doing that, but the weed didn't belong to me. The fact that she thought I did drugs and would even think of introducing something like that to Paul or Anna really hurt. It meant that she really had a very low opinion of me and that she'd never fully trust me. I mean, to a certain degree I could have lied about the stolen jewelry and said that I found it or something, but the pot I just couldn't explain. The only thing I knew for sure was that it didn't belong to me. But that didn't matter now because everyone in the house now viewed me as a drug user. I felt like I wanted to crawl under a rock and never show my face again.

After I washed my face and brushed my teeth I took a long look at myself in the mirror and was about to beat myself up some more when everything became clear.

"Maya!" I spoke her name. "Maya set me up. She's the one who put the weed in my bag and left it laying around so her mother would find it when she was cleaning up. Ugh!" I slapped my forehead with the palm of my hand. "Why didn't I see that it was Maya who did this to get even with me? That's why she told me to grow eyes in the back of my head. It was because she was always going to be in the shadows setting me up." I punched the palm of my left hand with my right fist a few times out of anger and revenge.

"Okay, Maya, you want to play like that," I murmured to myself. "If you want to play that dirty, then you got it! I'm going to be just as cruel!"

Later that day I found myself once again hanging out at the pool with Anna. I was fuming on the inside just waiting for the right opportunity to do what I needed to do. The usual suspects were there. Keysha was on duty. Maya was sitting on the other side reading, and there were a number of kids, teens and parents enjoying the weather and water.

"Are you okay?" Anna asked. "You seem really tense. I

know my mom came down really hard on you and all, but she'll forgive you. Trust me, I know."

"I'm cool, Anna," I said, remaining as calm, cool and collected as I could. I had a plan that I needed to execute and I was just waiting for the right moment.

"Okay, I was just making sure," she said as she relaxed and continued to sunbathe.

About twenty minutes went by before Carlo arrived. I tapped Anna and said, "Carlo is here."

"Really? Where?" Anna immediately sat upright and scanned the pool until she found him. As soon as Carlo entered the pool he walked directly over to Maya.

"Ugh, why doesn't she leave him alone? Why does she keep sending him mixed signals!" Anna grumbled.

"I won't tell you what I really think because she's your sister," I said.

"She's a freaking slut." Anna said it for me. "Look at her. She's freaking giving him the okay to rub suntan oil on her. What the hell!"

"Wait a minute, look over there." I pointed to the far right.

"Oh, here comes Misalo. Oh, I can't wait for him to see this," Anna said.

Misalo was on his cell phone talking to someone and wasn't really paying attention to what was happening on the pool deck.

"Oh, no! Aw, man!" Anna whined.

"What?" I asked.

"Look. Keysha must've spotted Misalo and is telling Carlo to stop."

"I really don't like her at all," I said, biting down on my bottom lip.

"And I really don't like the fact that Maya is toying with Carlo," Anna said. "Something needs to be done about that."

"You're right," I said as I reached for my cell phone and stood up.

"Where are you going?" Anna asked.

"Well, little cousin. Sometimes a girl has got to do what a girl has got to do. I'm about to go raise some hell."

"Wait! I'll walk with you. Carlo is leaving and I want to talk to him," Anna said.

Anna and I walked through the clubhouse and out onto the sidewalk. Anna rushed after Carlo while I waited to intercept Misalo.

"Hello." I smiled at him.

"Hi," he said and was about to continue on, but I stood in his path and got his full attention.

"Can I talk to you for a minute? It's really important," I said with a nice pretty-girl smile.

"Dude, let me holler back at you," Misalo said to the person he was talking to. He closed his phone and tucked it inside his front shirt pocket.

"What's up?" Misalo asked.

"You remember me, right? I'm Viviana, Maya's cousin."

"Yes, I know who you are," Misalo said.

"Good." I paused as I opened my cell phone and searched for the video clip I was looking for. "I know it's none of my business, but I thought you should know that Maya is playing you for a complete idiot."

"What are you talking about? Maya and I love each other. She'd never do anything to hurt me," Misalo said confidently.

"That's not entirely true. You see, the other night she and I were at a party together and she invited Carlo instead of you," I said, feeling justifiably wicked.

"Bull!" Misalo said, totally unconvinced that Princess Maya could do any wrong.

"I thought you might say that. Here, take a look." I showed Misalo the video of Maya and Carlo dancing together. The way she held on to him and the way she melted in Carlo's embrace when he started singing in her ear was too much for Misalo to take. He began pacing back and forth and calling Maya every name in the book. I got a twisted joy out of pulling Misalo's strings. I felt as if I were shooting my own personal episode of *Cheaters*.

"There is more," I said as I recalled the clip I'd just taken. I showed Maya allowing Carlo to put oil on her body and how they'd stopped when they knew Misalo was approaching.

"Oh, hell no! You've got to be freaking kidding me!" Misalo punched the palm of his left hand with his right fist.

"Wait a minute. Calm down," I said, placing one hand on his shoulder. I couldn't help it—the opportunity was there so I took it, and while slipping my hand into his shirt pocket I took out his phone. "If I were you I'd march onto the pool deck and let her have it!"

Misalo's chest heaved with anger and contempt. He'd turned into a scorned lover filled with jealousy, rage and betrayal. "Thank you, Viviana." Misalo hugged me briefly and then, like a shooting comet, rushed toward Maya. I stood smiling at the madness that I'd caused. I opened up Misalo's phone and to my delight it had not relocked itself yet. I took the liberty of scrolling through his pictures and was blown away when I came across several photos of Maya posing in her underwear.

"Oh, this is just too easy," I said, laughing to myself. "Maya, you truly are a tramp. So, you want to plant pot on me, aye. Well, let me show you how evil I can be." I attached her underwear photos to a text message and sent it to all of Misalo's contacts.

By the time I walked back onto the pool deck and took my seat, all hell had broken loose. Misalo was going ballistic. He had his finger pointed between her eyes. He looked as if he were about to pimp slap her. When Maya tried to move, he grabbed her and forced her into a seat. Maya couldn't charm her way out of her own deception. I took great joy in watching her run away from Misalo, crying uncontrollably. Keysha, being the dutiful friend she was, followed her. *I wonder if I can report her for leaving the pool unattended while people are still in the pool swimming,* I thought to myself as I powered Misalo's phone off. I rushed over to him so that I could return it.

"Hey, I'm really sorry, but I thought you should know," I said.

"Thank you," Misalo said as he swallowed hard.

"Look, you dropped your cell phone," I said as I handed it back to him.

"Thank you," he said once again before leaving.

# eighteen

MAYA

"Oh, my God, oh, my God, oh, my God." I kept repeating the phrase as I cried uncontrollably and rushed away from the swimming pool. Finally, I just stopped walking and collapsed to the ground and cried.

"Maya!" I heard Keysha calling me, but I didn't look in her direction. Keysha wrapped her arms around me and rocked me.

"I can't believe Misalo said all of those mean things to me," I cried. My heart was so broken. Misalo had said things that he could not take back. My heart was in so much pain.

"I know." Keysha tried to console me as she cried with me. "Love stinks sometimes," she said.

"I don't believe this, Keysha. Why? Why did Viviana do that?" I asked, but I knew she couldn't answer my questions.

"Come on. I need you to stand up," she said as she helped me get back to my feet. We walked back into the pool clubhouse and sat on one of the sofas.

"Why wouldn't Misalo even give me a chance to explain my side of the story before he went off on me?"

"I don't know. I think he was just hurt, Maya," Keysha said.

"What does all of this mean? Does he not trust me? Does he really think I'm a whore?" I asked as I continued to cry. Keysha held on to me, cried with me and stayed with me until I could shed no more tears.

I stayed with Keysha until she got off of work at 7:00 p.m. She then walked me home to make sure that I was okay. Keysha tried to keep my mind off my problems by talking about other things.

"What do you think about me dying my hair another color?" she asked as we slowly strolled along. I glanced at her.

"What color?" I asked.

"Strawberry," she said. I gave her a blank stare.

"No, you'd look crazy with strawberry hair," I said.

"I don't know. I think I have the right skin tone for a color that bold," she said, unwilling to admit the hair color would turn out to be a horrible disaster.

"I just want to go in the house and eat a gallon of peach-mango ice cream, and listen to sad love songs," I said before exhaling a long, depressing sigh. I thought about Misalo's hatred for me and started crying again.

Keysha and I briefly turned to glance behind us when we heard the wail of an ambulance siren approaching us. The noise it made was enough to give anyone a massive headache. Once the emergency vehicle zoomed past us, Keysha noticed that it had turned down my block.

"I wonder who is sick on your street?" she asked.

"Probably one of our elderly neighbors," I said, thinking about how good the ice cream was going to taste. We made the turn onto my block, and my heart nearly stopped beating when I saw the ambulance in my driveway.

"Oh, my God, Maya!" Keysha said as she and I both instinctively began running toward my house to see what had happened.

"Maya, get in the car," my father ordered before I could even ask him what was going on.

"What's happening?" I screamed nervously.

"Get in the car, Maya!" my father once again ordered. The next thing I saw was Anna unconscious and strapped down to the gurney and being wheeled to the back of the ambulance.

"What's going on?" I asked again.

"Maya, you should get in the car like your father said," Keysha said, pulling me over to the car. She opened the rear door and I got in.

"Call me and let me know if I can do anything," she said.

"I will," I said, watching my mom hop into the back of the emergency vehicle. Keysha closed the door and moved out of the way as my father rushed over and got into the driver's seat.

"Is she okay?" asked Viviana. I hadn't realized that she was already in the car.

"I don't know. I just don't know yet," I said as Dad put the car in Reverse and sped toward the hospital.

I sat in the emergency room with my family waiting to hear any news about Anna's condition. I didn't know if she was alive or dead. The only thing that we knew was that she came home, collapsed on the kitchen floor, had a seizure and became unresponsive. Both of my parents paced the floor nervously as we waited to hear news of her condition. My phone rang and I glanced down at the caller ID and saw that it was Keysha. I was about to answer the phone, but my mother walked over to me and said, "Give it to me." Without even asking her why, I did. She powered my phone off and tucked it in her purse. "Give me yours, too," she asked for Viviana's phone. "You both need to be focused on praying for Anna, not talking to your friends."

"What did you do to my sister?" I leaned over and whispered to Viviana, who was sitting next to me.

"You can't blame this one on me. I didn't do a damn thing," Viviana whispered back.

"Yes, you did! This drama has your name written all over it. Every place you and your mother go you cause chaos," I snarled at her.

"You can go to hell, Maya!" Viviana's voice boomed. My mother was on us quicker than funk on crap.

"I don't want to hear another damn word out of either of you!" My mother wasn't playing. I decided to leave Viviana alone for the time being.

Grandmother Esmeralda arrived as soon as she could and waited for any news along with the rest of us. It was well past midnight before a doctor came out to give us an update on Anna.

Tori Grant was the head doctor taking care of Anna. She was a decent-looking woman in her late thirties with brown shoulder-length hair, full rosy cheeks and a warm smile. Dr. Grant took us into a private room, where she began explaining what had happened.

"I'm going to be very frank with everyone and let you know that Anna nearly died tonight." We all gasped.

"She's not out of the woods yet, but I'm confident she'll make it," Dr. Grant explained.

"What happened to my baby?" my mother asked.

"Mrs. Rogers, are you aware that your daughter has been using meth?"

"No, Anna doesn't do drugs. No one in our house does drugs," my father said, absolutely positive of this fact.

"Well, Mr. Rogers, I hate to tell you this but Anna is." The room grew silent.

"Anna overdosed on meth, which caused her to have a seizure and her kidneys began to fail." I was in total shock.

"Do you have any idea where she got it?" asked Dr. Grant. No one said a word but my mother, grandmother, father and I all looked at Viviana and passed judgment on her right then and there.

"It wasn't me. I swear it on my father's grave. I don't know where she got it." Viviana immediately denied having anything to do with this incident. Dr. Grant went on to say, "Sometimes meth overdoses are a suicide attempt. Inexperienced meth users may overdose because they are not sure how much meth they need to get high, while more experienced users often develop a tolerance to the drug and need more of it to get high, resulting in an overdose. Because street meth is often cooked in illegal labs, its composition can vary from one batch to another. This means that every time a person uses meth the drug will be different. A person who has used meth before without overdosing can use the same amount again and suffer an overdose, because the meth contained different concentrations of chemicals. A person who has overdosed on meth may not be immediately aware of it. Once symptoms do appear they can progress rapidly to death. As the drug begins to affect their body, it may cause symptoms such as dilated pupils, hyperthermia, dehydration characterized by dry mouth and lips, and lack of urination. They can also experience chest pain, difficulty breathing, muscle twitches, seizures, hallucinations or go into a coma."

"Oh, Jesus!" My father pressed his back against the wall and squatted down. This news literally knocked him off his feet.

"I think Anna was lucky this time. We're treating all of her symptoms. We're giving her medication to stop the convulsions, rehydrating her and looking for signs of any damage. So far she's responding well."

"When will we be able to see her?" asked Grandmother Esmeralda.

"We've got her sedated now. She probably won't be able to communicate with anyone for a few days. She's been moved to intensive care. Once they have her all settled in, I'll have someone come down and get you."

For the next two days, my family hung out at the hospital. We went home in shifts, but only stayed long enough to shower, change our clothes and head on back. When Anna finally did come out of the woods and open her eyes, my father, my mother, Viviana and I were in the room. The first thing she did was look at my father and smile. He held her hand and smiled back.

"How are you doing?" he asked.

"Okay," she said. "But I could use something to drink."
My mother brought Anna a cup of water, which she sipped
slowly.

"Anna, baby." My mother stepped around so that Anna
could see her. "I need you to tell me something and I want
the truth." Anna nodded her head, agreeing. My mother
glanced at Viviana briefly and then back at Anna.

"Where did you get the drugs that you took?" she asked.
Anna closed her eyes and started crying.

"I'm sorry, Mom. The pot you found in Viviana's bag was
mine. I didn't smoke it—it was just given to me."

"Was the person who gave you the pot the same person
who gave you the meth?" my mother asked.

"I didn't know it was meth. I took it without asking,"
Anna said, crying.

"Okay, honey, where did you get it?" My mother pressed
Anna for the truth.

"At Carlo's house. His cousin gave me the pot. I don't
know why I kept it. I just stuck it in Viviana's things until I
could get rid of it."

I glanced over at Viviana and she'd turned pale, looking
as if she'd just been kicked in the gut by a mule.

"Anna." My mother made Anna look at her. "Did Carlo
force you over to his house?" Anna turned her head and met
my gaze. I could see tears in her eyes.

"No," she whispered. The room was silent for a long a
moment. "Please don't make me say it."

"Were you having sex with this boy?" my mother asked.

Anna's tears began flowing, "No, we came close but I got
scared."

"Why, Anna?" My father looked even more wounded than when he'd seen the photo of Misalo and me making out. The lines in his forehead seemed to have gotten deeper within the past few hours.

"I wanted him to like me more than he did Maya," Anna confessed, turned her face into the pillow and sobbed.

When I got home that evening all I wanted to do was take a shower and crawl into my bed. Viviana, my grandmother and father all remained at the hospital with Anna. As soon as my mother and I entered the house I asked her if I could have my cell phone back. She reached into her purse and handed it to me as she walked off toward her bedroom. I took a shower, put on my pj's, crawled into bed and immediately went to sleep. Waking up the next morning the first thing I did was reach for my cell phone. I turned it on and watched as a slew of text messages and voice mails appeared. Most of them were from Keysha. I sat upright in my bed and gave her a call.

"Hey, girl," I said when she answered.

"Maya! Oh, my God, girl. Is Anna okay? What happened to her?" Keysha sounded as if the world was ending.

"It's a long story, but to answer your question, Anna is going to be just fine," I said.

"I've got nothing but time." Keysha offered a willing ear.

"No, really. She's going to be okay." I exhaled as my mind drifted to thoughts of Misalo.

"Are you sure?" Keysha asked once again.

"Yes, I'm positive," I answered.

"Well, at least that's some good news because, girl, you've got a big problem," she informed me.

"Keysha, I don't need any more problems," I griped. "I have to figure out how to make up with Misalo."

"I'm not sure that's going to be all that easy," Keysha said.

"Huh? What are you talking about?"

"Maya, I don't know how to tell you this so I'm just going to say it."

"Keysha, what is it?" I wanted to get to the point.

"Misalo has snapped on you."

"You're still not making any sense to me," I said.

"Did you take some pictures of yourself in your underwear and send them to him?" When Keysha asked me that I swear I thought time had frozen and the world had stopped spinning.

"I'll take the silence to mean yes. I don't like being the one to tell you this, but he forwarded your pictures and a mean text message to all of his friends. Everyone in the neighborhood is talking about you, Maya. All of your personal business is in the street."

★ ★ ★ ★ ★

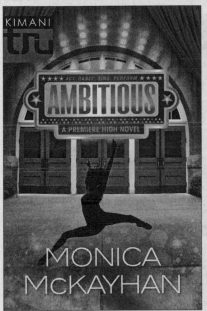

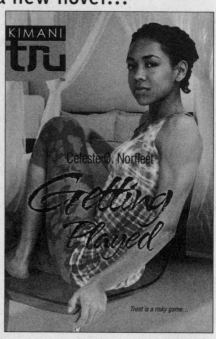

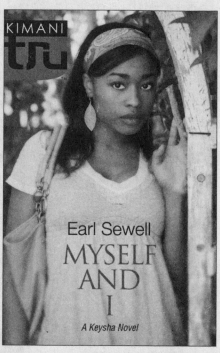